Tunes
for a
Small Harmonica

An Ursula Nordstrom Book

Tunes
for a
Small Harmonica

a novel by Barbara Wersba

Harper & Row, Publishers
New York, Hagerstown, San Francisco, London

The lines on pages 24, 27, and 30 are taken from How to Play the Marine Band Type Harmonica *by Sigmund Spaeth, Catalog No. HT-3. Copyright © 1971 by M. Hohner Co. Reprinted by permission.*

The poem on page 44 is from Collected Poems of Charlotte Mew, *published by Gerald Duckworth & Co., Ltd., 3, Henrietta Street, London, W.C.2, 1953. Reprinted by permission.*

The poem on page 143 is from Poems, 1920–1945 *by David Morton, published by Alfred A. Knopf, Inc., New York, 1945. Reprinted by permission.*

Library of Congress Cataloging in Publication Data
Wersba, Barbara.
    Tunes for a small harmonica.

    SUMMARY: A rebellious New York teenager, having fallen in love with her poetry teacher, plans to rescue him from poverty.
    I. Title.
PZ7.W473Tu   [Fic]   75–25411
ISBN 0–06–026372–5
ISBN 0–06–026373–3 lib. bdg.

Tunes
for a
Small Harmonica

An Ursula Nordstrom Book

1

It all began because I fell in love with a person named Harold Murth. I did not want to fall in love with Harold Murth—in fact, I did not even like him. But I fell in love with him when I was sixteen and he was thirty, and he changed my life.

Harold Murth was a very pale person. His hair was pale, his face was pale, his clothes were pale—and when he spoke, the words became pale. He taught poetry at the private school I attended in New York, and the only reason Marylou and I signed up for his class was because he was a man. There were exactly two male teachers at Miss Howlett's School for Girls, and since the other was an eighty-year-old Russian who taught Slavic Languages, our choice was Harold. But who would have known that Harold Murth would be so dull? The minute he opened his mouth and said, "Poems are the wings of the mind," I fell asleep.

Marylou was more compassionate about him because she was more compassionate about everything. She was the type of person who was always finding diseased kittens on the street and rushing them to the SPCA—and the type of person who could say of the ugliest girl in school, "Yes, but she has a lovely *smile.*" Marylou made an absolutely terrific friend, because her loyalties were extreme. If you had the flu she would fight her way through a snowstorm to bring you a hot toddy in a thermos, and if you were broke she would not only loan you her allowance but go to the bank and withdraw her savings. She was a straight-A student, whereas I was lucky to get C's, and had a photographic memory of unlikely documents—such as maps of Yugoslavia.

Marylou's temperament made up for her looks, which consisted mostly of some limp bangs, a crooked smile and ten bitten fingernails. She was usually to be seen wearing oxfords and a shabby camel's-hair coat—a book on archaeology under her arm. For, beyond the shadow of a doubt, she believed that she would one day be digging holes in Egypt.

I, on the other hand, had never been famous for my disposition. I was usually in a bad mood, late for appointments, and suffered from constant cigaret hangovers. I refused to study, hated going to private school, and thought of myself as a revolutionary. Very tough. Very hard. As a matter of fact, I had once led a revolution— a long campaign to liberate every girl at Miss Howlett's from wearing the school uniform. Here we all were, in the mid-1960's, wearing pleated skirts and blue blazers when the rest of New York was letting itself fall apart in faded Levi's and sandals. Men in long hair and beads. Girls going bra-less down Madison Avenue. Pot parties among the middle-aged. I lost the battle, of course, but my fame became rampant in the lower grades and it was not long before shy seventh and eighth graders were passing me in the halls and saying breathlessly, "Hi there, J.F."

My name was—and still is—Jacqueline Frances McAllister, but I had been called J.F. from the age of twelve when I had decided to dress like a boy for the rest of my life. (Oh God, such wonderful memories of Army-Navy Stores, seamen's sweaters and khaki raincoats, rough corduroy pants, white athletic socks. Heavy sneakers. Terrycloth bathrobes for five dollars.) I must confess that this was the only thing that ever drove my mother to see a psychiatrist. My mother was the height of coolness, but she simply could not conceive of owning the toughest kid on the block—especially when the block was Park Avenue and the kid was a girl. "Do nothing," the psychiatrist said. "It is a form of acting out. She will get over it." But I did not get over it, and by the age of fifteen I was a kind of transvestite. I could walk down the loneliest street in New York without being attacked, and the minute I set foot in Central Park a gang of boys was asking me to join a baseball game.

All of which, naturally enough, made me think I was gay—so off I went to the library. The library had hundreds of books on this intricate topic (*I Was a Homosexual Evangelist*; *The Homosexual in New Zealand*; *Homosexuality and Low Blood Sugar*) and it took me weeks to browse through. Quite frankly, I was amazed. Who would have thought such things went on? I found them terribly interesting, but could not imagine myself partaking of

3

them. So as an experiment I went over to Marylou's house and suggested that we neck. Marylou—the epitome of kindness—tried to adjust herself to the idea.

"You mean you want to kiss me?"

"Well yes, Marylou. If you wouldn't mind."

"Oh. Well. All right. But why are we doing it?"

"As an experiment. Just think of it as research."

"J.F., I am your best friend, and I will *always* be your best friend, but . . ."

"One kiss, Marylou. In the name of science."

We kissed passionately and I felt nothing. It was a terrible disappointment. I went back to the library and read some more. To tell you the truth, the whole thing was beginning to turn me off, but since I had never been one to admit defeat I decided to march in a Gay Lib parade and see how *that* felt. Perhaps it would engender a sense of community.

The parade was being sponsored by the Manhattan Chapter of the Greater New York Homophile Alliance— and the participants were supposed to gather at 96th Street and march down Fifth Avenue. I gathered, and was instantly appalled at the people I was going to march with. I was also shocked at my own reaction. Where was my revolutionary spirit? And the parade itself was a disaster because no sooner had we gone one block in strict formation, singing "We Shall Overcome," when I saw my mother's best friend Tippy Bernhardt standing on the corner of 95th. She was waving frantically for a cab, and seemed to turn into stone the minute she saw me. Her arm,

4

raised to hail the cab, became suspended over her head and a glassy smile froze on her face. She looked like the Statue of Liberty. Panic-stricken, I decided to make the best of a bad situation and threw my arm around the shoulders of the fat lady marching next to me. Two boys in front of us were holding hands and a minister was carrying a huge sign that said GAY IS GOOD. I smiled and nodded as we passed poor Tippy, and had the strange impression that she would remain that way forever, frozen like Galatea, timelessly denied the comfort and convenience of a cab.

Frankly, I would have preferred being gay. Because now that I knew I wasn't, I had no earthly idea of what I was. "A eunuch?" I asked Marylou.

"No, J.F. Eunuchs are men."

"Then maybe I'm a hermaphrodine."

"Hermaphro*dite*," Marylou corrected. "You couldn't be. That's someone who is both sexes at once."

"I'm not even pretty," I said.

Marylou looked at me in surprise. "But you are! Well, not exactly pretty. But . . . handsome."

We stared at each other. Because this, precisely, was the problem. I—a heterosexual female—looked exactly like a very young Steve McQueen. And I still had so many eccentric habits, like carrying a Swiss Army Knife in my pocket at all times, that I despaired of ever fitting into the scheme of things.

The fact that I did not *want* to fit into the scheme of things was the conundrum. On the one hand I was a rebel,

5

and on the other hand I was a nervous wreck. Dedicated to dressing like a boy, I derived no inner peace from dressing like a boy. (And here I must digress to pound the message home that I did not dress like other boys. No love beads or bell-bottom pants for me. No leather sandals bought in the Village. No pseudo-hippie Indian shirts. No. It was all corduroy and Windbreakers and white sweat shirts a size too large.) But there seemed to be no other choice. I looked ridiculous in girl's clothes, and unless I wore my hair very short and slicked back I tended to resemble one of Jesus' disciples. All of which brings me to the subject of Dr. Waingloss.

Dr. Waingloss was an eclectic, and it must have taken me five months before I knew what the word meant. Our family doctor had suggested to my mother that I see him, and so I started therapy in the beginning of my junior year at Miss Howlett's. His office was on Central Park West and 70th Street and always smelled of bananas. He was not a Freudian with a Viennese accent, nor was he Jungian, Existential, Interpersonal or Transactional. Dr. Waingloss was simply eclectic—and thus plagiarized everyone.

"Are you, uh . . . a Freudian or something?" I asked him during my first visit.

Dr. Waingloss smiled. "Why do you ask that, J.F.?"

"I don't know. I was just wondering."

"Have you read much about Freud?"

"No. Not really."

"Jung?"

"No, actually I haven't."

6

"Then why do you ask?"

"I don't know," I said. "I just wondered what you were."

"Let us talk about what *you* are," Dr. Waingloss said kindly. "Your clothes interest me enormously. Do you always dress like that?"

And do you always eat bananas? I wanted to ask him. And do you always smile that sickly smile before you ask a question? Why are there no diplomas hanging on your walls? Where are your credentials?

"Maybe you're Existential," I said to him hopefully. "R.D. Laing and stuff like that."

Dr. Waingloss nodded. "You are familiar with Laing?"

"Well, no. But I read an article about him once. In a magazine."

"Tell me about your chain-smoking," said Dr. Waingloss. "What is it? Two packs a day?"

"Three," I replied. "Where did you go to school? In the East?"

Dr. Waingloss leaned back in his lounge-chair. His eyes were bloodshot and there was a small stain on his tie. "You seem mistrustful of me, J.F. Shall we talk about it?"

Mistrustful? I thought. I wouldn't trust you if I were drowning in a vat of olive oil.

"It's just that I was curious about you," I said politely. "I mean, I find it quite interesting. The education of psychiatrists."

"What surfaces about trusting people?" he asked. "What comes up?"

"I beg your pardon?"

7

"What comes to the surface of your mind when I say the word 'trust'?"

"Perhaps you are from the West," I said to him. "California."

Dr. Waingloss smiled and began to write on a pad with the stub of a pencil—and from that moment on I despised him. There were days when I was afraid that I would do him bodily harm, and days when I felt that if he said, "What comes up?" one more time I would shove a banana down his throat.

Dr. Waingloss' eclecticism was a great convenience to him, because it meant that he was never required to make sense. One day he would speak of Transference, and the next he would discuss our Interpersonal Relationship. On Monday he would talk of Transactions and on Thursday of my Electra Complex. But I could have borne all this fraudulence if only the man had had a vestige of personal hygiene. (Horrid Dr. Waingloss. To this day I can see you sitting in your leather lounge-chair, your clothes never entirely clean, your fingernails always bearing a faint black line. You were physically revolting, yet spoke in smooth and honeyed tones—like an educated snake. You wrote your secret notes about me with a nasty little pencil stub and were always sneezing into a soiled handkerchief.)

I sat at the dinner table that night—after my first session with Dr. Waingloss—and stared at my plate. I had no appetite for the filet mignon, or the asparagus with hollandaise, or the strawberries soaked in Cointreau. Bertha, our housekeeper, was annoyed and yanked the plates away with a vengeance. My mother had been watching me for a half hour, waiting for me to say something. But I was mute.

"Well," she said finally. "How did it go?"

"How did what go?"

"The *session*," she said impatiently.

"With Dr. Waingloss?"

"Of course with Dr. Waingloss! Who else?"

"It was OK," I replied.

"Did you like him?"

"Oh, yes," I said. "A lot."

"He's supposed to be terribly good," she said defensively.

"He is," I assured her. "Terrific."

"Are you being serious, Jacqueline?"

"Yes. I am. He's a genius."

"What did you talk about?"

"I'm not supposed to say. It's private."

My mother nodded grudgingly and returned to her strawberries. I figured that since she would send me to Dr. Waingloss anyway, I might as well make her feel that she was getting her money's worth. After I had marched in the Gay Lib parade, the ultimatum had been announced. Either I go to Dr. Waingloss for a year or be yanked out of school and deposited at the Stonington Retreat—a place for disturbed teen-agers. Needless to say, I had chosen Dr. Waingloss.

We made an odd couple at the table every night—me in my Steve McQueen outfit and my mother in a velvet hostess gown. Her hair had been done at George Michael's that day, her nails at Elizabeth Arden, and her figure toned up by a French masseuse. Which was the interesting thing about my mother. Every part of her came from a different place. I had thought of her in sections for so long —hair, nails, feet, waistline—that it was difficult to see her as an integrated being.

Then there was the matter of her clothes, for which five closets had been built in the apartment. Her Manhattan clothes were bought at Bergdorf Goodman, and her Southampton clothes came from Abercrombie & Fitch. Her Europe clothes were purchased at Saks Fifth Avenue, while her shoes and bags came from Lord & Taylor. I forget where her nightgowns and slips descended from, but I have the odd impression that they were made by a cloistered order of nuns. In Belgium.

Every day my mother and Tippy Bernhardt did the same thing. In the morning they shopped for two hours at one of the above stores. Then they would have lunch in a little bistro off Fifth Avenue, where they would discuss their friends' divorces. After that each of them would depart for a session with a masseuse, hairdresser or manicurist. On Saturdays they went to an exclusive gym and "worked out," and on Sundays they read the clothing ads in the *Times* and talked to each other on the phone. It was a perfect friendship.

As for my father, who worked for Standard Oil, we never saw him. He was always in conference, and until I was eight years old I had thought that conference was a place, like London or Paris. "My father is in Conference," I would say to kids in my class, with the air of someone whose parent is extremely mysterious and well-travelled. Then one day I had learned that he was simply downtown in his office, too busy to come home.

My mother finished her strawberries and gazed at herself in the mirror over the sideboard. There were candles on the table that night, which softened her expression a little. "Do you like my hair?" she asked. "They did it differently today."

I looked at her and saw that the question was rhetorical. She was much too busy studying herself to expect a reply.

"Yeah," I said. "It looks fine."

I got up from the table and went to my room. I had a new Judy Collins record and was anxious to play it. But the minute I turned on the hi-fi I realized that I didn't want to play it at all. Nor did I want to phone Marylou, or do my homework, or read the latest edition of *You and Your Bike*—a manual of do-it-yourself repairs.

There was nothing I wanted to do.

I sat on the bed and looked at my room, which had been decorated by my mother to resemble the boudoir of an aging debutante. Everything in it was pink and blue, like the frosting on a birthday cake, and there was a fussy dressing table that had perfume bottles on it and a collection of glass mice. My real possessions—such as my ten-speed bicycle, my racing skates and hockey sticks—were kept isolated, like lepers, in the basement of our building. My sled was there too, a relic of days long past, and my

professional archery set. A man named Winthrop Honeycomb, who was my father's best friend, had given me that
for my twelfth birthday. It was the best present I ever got.

I tried to remember being twelve.

But all I could think of was Dr. Waingloss and how we
were about to spend a year together, Mondays and Thursdays. One year of stale bananas and evasions. A year of
other people's cigaret smoke hovering in the air, and the
venetian blinds closed against the world, and his horrid
little pencil scribbling secret words about my neurosis.
One solid year of wondering whether he was Freudian or
Jungian.

2

I am not yet ready to plunge into the story of Harold Murth. There are other things to tell, without which Harold's saga will be meaningless. I must, for example, discuss Marylou in greater detail, her parents and little brother Nelson—and how I learned to play the harmonica. The harmonica is important here because it connects with Harold's poverty, our relationship, and the amazing things that happened thereafter.

To begin with, Marylou's parents were different from mine. I am tempted to say that they were another species. Whereas my parents were rich, conventional and Republican, Marylou's father and mother were playwrights who slept till noon, had bearded friends and lived in the moment. When times were good they had a maid and went to opening nights and bought their kids presents. When times were bad they wrote soap operas in their West Side apartment, fired the maid and drank too much. In the period I am discussing, times were very bad.

Marylou took care of her parents as though some malignant fairy had decided that she would be the parent and they the children. Every morning of her life she got up at six, made a meat loaf or casserole for dinner, dressed

13

Nelson for school, put him on the bus, left a pot of coffee on the stove for her still-sleeping parents—and then went to school. Every afternoon of her life Marylou collected Nelson at his private school, came home, tidied up the apartment, went out to get groceries or pick up the laundry, gave everyone their supper, put Nelson to bed, and then—around ten o'clock—started her homework. And she never even complained. It was undoubtedly her idea of the nature of life that one should be of service to people. And it drove me mad.

"Why do you *do* all that stuff?" I would yell at her. "Don't you know they're using you?"

"J.F.," she would reply calmly, "they are my parents. I love them."

I would look at her thin little face and skimpy brown bangs and feel very sad, very helpless. For it was evident that Marylou wasn't going to change. She would go on being of service to people for the rest of her life—and if anyone took advantage of her she wouldn't care. What I found particularly baffling was how proper she was. Here were Samuel and Bradley Brown—her parents—living in their pajamas and staying up all night writing plays while Marylou wore her school uniform even on Saturdays and had perfect manners. She rose to her feet every time an adult entered the room and opened doors for old ladies without even thinking about it. She was always giving her seat to people on the bus and—without fail—used the right fork for desserts, while I absentmindedly used a spoon.

Two days after my session with Dr. Waingloss Marylou asked me to come over to her house after school. She said that she had a present for me, a statement which aroused no small amount of interest in my heart. Marylou gave the best presents of anyone I knew. It was she who had given me my Swiss Army Knife, my track shoes, my barometer, and—one of my very best things—a boy's wool jacket with the words "Tappan Zee High School" on the back. (The history of this garment is interesting, Marylou having found it in the middle of Central Park one day while taking her brother for a walk. There, abandoned on a wooden bench was the wondrous jacket, the words "Tappan Zee High School" emblazoned on the back in gold. Being as honest as a saint, Marylou had sat with the jacket for two hours, waiting to see if anyone would claim it. When no one did, she had scooped it up and brought it over to my house. It fit perfectly.)

At three o'clock that day we dashed downstairs to the lockers—I to change from my hated school uniform into Levi's and sweat shirt, and Marylou to get her umbrella. Then, in a drizzling rain, we set out on foot for Nelson's school on 84th Street. He was waiting for us in front of the big black doors and grinned wildly as he saw us approach.

"Hi, Marylou! Hi, J.F. It's raining!"

"J.F. has a headache," said Marylou, taking his hand. "So try to be quiet Nelson, please."

I flashed Marylou a grateful glance. For, though I did not have a headache, I could hardly bear Nelson's manic cheerfulness. Marylou had once told me that he went to sleep smiling every night and woke up smiling every morning—which made me want to puke. Nelson was without a doubt the Hubert Humphrey of the first grade.

We proceeded west across Central Park in stony silence, Nelson giving little skips every now and then and flashing an angelic smile at his sister. "I won a spelling contest today," he said in an elaborate whisper. "I was the best."

"For God's sake, Nelson!" I said. "You don't have to whisper!"

"But you have a headache," he whispered.

"I do not have a headache. I have a brain tumor. So shout all you want."

A look of distress crossed Nelson's face. "Does she really have a brain tumor?" he asked Marylou.

"No. Of course not."

He brightened at once. "That's good. Because I won a spelling contest today and . . ."

By the time we reached Marylou's apartment I really did have a headache, so we deposited Nelson in his room —where he could watch the afternoon movie on TV—and headed down the hall. From the bedroom we could hear Bradley Brown typing next week's installment of *The Secret Holocaust*—a soap opera. Samuel Brown was nowhere to be seen.

"What ho?" said a voice from the den. We looked in and saw Mr. Brown, still in his pajamas, sitting on the floor. He was drinking scotch and reading a copy of *Playboy.* "Hi," he said.

"Hi," we both said back.

16

"Come in," he said warmly. "Have a drink."

"Daddy, you know we don't drink," said Marylou.

"Well, come in anyway. I'm lonesome. I need company."

Marylou gazed at the bottle of scotch. "Bad news?"

"Couldn't be worse," said Mr. Brown. "He dropped the option. The bastard simply dropped it."

The bastard Mr. Brown was speaking of was William L. Williams, a theatrical producer who had been holding one of Mr. Brown's plays under option for a year. The Browns had believed that this play would be produced on Broadway and had put some money down on a Fire Island house in anticipation of the event. Now—as with most of Mr. Brown's plays—the option had been dropped.

Marylou was sympathetic about these option-droppings, but I was not because I had personally read all of Samuel Brown's plays and thought they stank. And despite the fact that Marylou typed every one of them with religious fervor, she knew how bad they were too. Each new play by Samuel Brown resembled a play by someone else, so that you never knew whether you were reading Tennessee Williams, Arthur Miller, William Inge, or all of them rolled together. As a classic example, I remember a play of Mr. Brown's called *Death of a Dentist* in which the entire action takes place during a picnic in the French Quarter of New Orleans. The dentist is a drug addict, and his wife keeps telling everyone that attention should be paid to him. In the end he commits suicide by taking an overdose of novocaine.

17

"The bastard," Mr. Brown repeated. "He simply dropped it."

"I'm so sorry," said Marylou.

"What a phony," said Samuel Brown. "He takes you to thirty-dollar lunches for a whole year, sends you tickets to openings, phones you in the middle of the night from London or some goddamn place, sends your wife flowers on her birthday—and then he *drops the goddamn option.* It's too much."

"I'm so sorry," Marylou said again.

"But do you know what I hate about him most?" Mr. Brown queried a large, invisible audience. "The thing I hate about him most is that he pretends to be cultivated. A connoisseur of wine, an expert on the eighteenth century, a collector of rare books. And do you know where he made his money? Laundry detergent."

"We have to do our homework," I lied to Mr. Brown. "I'm sorry about your option."

Marylou leaned down and kissed her father on the cheek. "Don't worry, Daddy. Tomorrow will be better."

"Laundry detergent," Mr. Brown mumbled as we left the den.

(It occurs to me to mention here that Bradley Brown's plays were of an entirely different order. Spare, blunt and abstract, they had interesting one-word titles like *Bucket* and *Trolley* and were always set on a bare stage with the back wall of the theatre showing. One of them, called *Spoon*, had been produced in a regional theatre in Boston and Marylou and I had taken the train up to see it.

18

Though totally incomprehensible, the play had held my interest because the two characters in it—there were only two—had been stark naked the whole time and had spent three acts arguing over a large spoon. I thought it was terrible that when hard times came it was always Bradley Brown who wrote the soap operas while Samuel Brown wallowed in self-pity and scotch.)

We went into Marylou's room, shut the door and collapsed on the bed. Her room was considerably better than mine—since she had decorated it herself—and was adorned with travel posters and Mexican glass. Her collection of archaeology books lined an entire wall.

"Here," she said, producing a small present from a bureau drawer. It was beautifully wrapped in gold paper.

I held it in my hand. "You give terrific presents," I said.

"You haven't even opened it, J.F."

"I know, but I just wanted to say that. All the presents you give are nice."

At that moment the door opened and Nelson burst into the room. "Bette Davis is on television!" he announced. "*Dark Victory!*"

I have forgotten to mention that Nelson was obsessed with old movies. He watched them every afternoon.

"Not now, dear," said Marylou.

"But it's so *good*," he pleaded. "Watch it for just five minutes."

"In a little while," said Marylou. "I promise."

"Now about this present," she said, when Nelson had departed. "It's connected with your smoking, and I want you to give it very serious thought."

I stared at her. "My smoking?"

"Yes. Because, J.F., you are now smoking three packs a day and it's ruining your wind. Remember how you won the hockey cup two years ago? You couldn't do that now. You barely have wind enough to ride your bike."

"Well . . ."

"Don't you care about your wind? You used to be so athletic."

"Well, I care and I don't care. If you know what I mean."

"I do know what you mean, but you have to make some kind of an effort. Why are you destroying yourself?"

I sat there for a moment, trying to answer this question. But nothing came to mind.

There was a knock on the door and Bradley Brown walked in. She was wearing her pajamas.

"Girls," she said, "I have a problem. I can't decide whether Marcia should have a breakdown and go to a sanatorium, or have a terrible car accident. What do you think?"

She sat down on the bed with us and ran a hand through her hair. Mrs. Brown was very small and young and pretty —and Marcia was one of her characters in *The Secret Holocaust.* The actress who played this part had a slight drinking problem, and whenever she seemed ready to go on a binge Mrs. Brown removed her from the script.

"I think she should go to a sanatorium," said Marylou. "Don't you, J.F.?"

"I don't know," I said. "Wasn't she in a sanatorium before?"

"No," Mrs. Brown explained. "The time before she was on a religious retreat. In Canada."

"With Dr. Bob?" I asked.

"No, no, J.F. With the lapsed priest—Father Paul."

It was all coming back to me. Marcia had divorced Dr. Bob in order to marry Father Paul—only Father Paul had had a stroke in the middle of the ceremony. This event had caused Marcia to convert to Catholicism, and we were now at the point where both she and Dr. Bob were nursing Father Paul back to health.

"I've got it," I said. "Maybe Father Paul didn't have a stroke. Maybe it was some rare disease he caught in the tropics a long time ago. When he was a missionary. Now Marcia has caught this disease too, and has to go out west for treatment. It could be a recurring disease—then you could get rid of her whenever you want."

Mrs. Brown gazed at me. "J.F., you are too much."

"I beg your pardon?"

"It's good. I'm going to use it."

Marylou smiled. "J.F. should have been a writer."

"Hell no," I said, embarrassed.

"Many thanks," said Mrs. Brown, heading for the door. She turned back. "J.F., I am mad about your sweat shirt."

I blushed. My sweat shirt had "Down With Reality" printed on it. I had bought it in Times Square.

When we were alone again Marylou said, "You better open your present, or somebody else will come in."

21

I tore off the paper and opened an oblong box. Inside was a harmonica.

Marylou looked a little worried. "Do you like it?"

My mind raced madly, but I couldn't think of a thing to say. It was the worst present she had ever given me.

"It's a harmonica," I said. And then there was a silence.

"It isn't just a harmonica," Marylou said testily. "It is a means to an end."

I looked at her, baffled.

"It requires a lot of wind to play the harmonica," she explained. "Smokers can't play them. So if you become a harmonica player you'll have to stop smoking. It's as basic as that."

"Oh."

Marylou had her face turned away from me. She seemed very tense. "You see, J.F., while I know you never think about it, I love you. And I don't want you to die of lung cancer."

"I think about it," I said.

"So I'd like you to promise me to play this instrument. There are instructions in the box."

I looked at my harmonica. It had "Marine Band" stamped on it. It was weird. "OK," I said. "I'll try. And I really appreciate the thought, Marylou."

For one moment Marylou became someone else. Someone older, and very tired. "No, you don't appreciate it. You don't appreciate anything. But it doesn't matter— just learn to play it."

The door opened and Nelson erupted into the room. He

had a cookie in one hand and a bottle of Schweppes Tonic in the other. "Bette Davis is going blind!" he said. "It's so *good*!"

And that was when—for no reason at all—I lost my temper. "Nelson," I said, "there is something I have wanted to tell you for years. You are a creep. A total, unrelieved creep."

A tear the size of a huge raindrop rolled down Nelson's face. But I did not care.

3

"Pick up your harmonica and hold it with the numbers up and facing you," said the instruction booklet. "There are ten holes altogether. This refers to the basic harmonica of ten single holes. Other harmonicas with extended musical ranges can have as many as twelve or fourteen single holes. For a start you need only the four numbered 4, 5, 6, and 7. With these you can produce a complete scale from C to C, a total of eight notes."

I lit a cigaret and gazed at my harmonica. It was the most useless thing I had ever owned—with the exception, perhaps, of a Water Pollution Kit that Nelson had given me one Christmas. You were supposed to insert this strange device under the water tap, fill it halfway up, pour in a packet of green powder, and thus discover to what degree you were being poisoned by the city water system. Then there had been the Weather Radio that I had bought on impulse at Korvette's, only to discover that it did not give the weather at all, but a demented stream of static. Now I owned a harmonica. And it was a foregone conclusion that I would never play it, for I was not musical.

I sat at my dressing table and stared at the collection of glass mice. Was I musical? Five years earlier my father's great-aunt had died and left us nothing but an upright piano. Bitterly resentful, my mother had placed it in the den and forgotten about it. But I, when no one was home, had begun to pick out pieces like "London Bridge" and "Silent Night" and had rather enjoyed it. Within a month I was playing dozens of tunes by ear, and might have made further progress had not my mother discovered me one afternoon and phoned for a piano teacher on the spot. A day later the dreadful woman arrived—a red-haired spinster named Doris Villanelle—and almost as quickly my musical talent disappeared. I became tone-deaf and stupid, depressed and mute, as Miss Villanelle sat by my side, metronome ticking, whispering "*One*-two-three, *one*-two-three," into my right ear. It was a ghastly experience and Miss Villanelle had eventually quit, using the dishonest excuse that she did not wish to teach piano to a female child who chewed bubble gum and dressed like a boy.

Besides the harmonica there were two things that were depressing me very much—and the first one was that I had called Nelson a creep. The fact that he *was* a creep was no excuse for hurting his feelings, and I could not imagine why I had done so. The second thing that was depressing me was that Marylou thought I was unappreciative. In other words, all her years of love and devotion seemed for naught.

I considered this hard and long, trying to decide if I was a person who did not appreciate things—and to my horror, decided that I was exactly that type of person. I was spoiled and had never known it before. People were kind to me and I did not care.

I thought about phoning Marylou, but then glanced at

the clock and saw that it was almost time for my second session with Dr. Waingloss—quarter of five. I would have to take a cab. Rushing into the hall I collided with a large man dressed in a dark gray suit, and was just about to apologize when I realized that it was my father. He seemed startled too.

"J.F.!" he said. "How are you?"

We shook hands. "Fine," I said. "Fine." I had not seen him for weeks.

"You look . . ." my father began. He paused and gazed at me. "Well," he concluded. "Very well."

"I am well," I replied.

"How's everything going?"

"Fine," I said.

"Great," he said. "Have you seen your mother?"

I searched my mind. It was Thursday, so she was probably at George Michael's. "The hairdresser," I said.

My father grinned sheepishly. "There's an elevator strike downtown. The office had to close."

"Great," I said. "Well, I have to go now."

"Good to see you, J.F.," said my father.

"Me too," I said. "Great."

(A pause should be taken here to describe my father, who was an interesting man inasmuch as he typified so many things American. To begin with he had gone to Princeton and still wore a crew cut, though we were now well into the 1960's. Secondly, he gravitated between his office and his club, was only comfortable with men exactly like himself, and read *The Wall Street Journal* as if it were a daily document from Mount Olympus. He was staunchly Republican, drank only the best scotch, played squash on Saturdays and was charming to women without really liking them. The breadth and vision of his mind might well be explained by saying that when the Watergate scandal broke in the early 70's my father came to the conclusion that Richard Nixon had been drugged by Bob Haldeman. "Tranquilizers," my father said firmly. "They gave the poor guy tranquilizers. No wonder he's erratic." This was, if nothing else, at least an original explanation of our country's moral collapse and it stuck in my mind like glue.)

On the way to Dr. Waingloss' office I leaned back in the taxi and studied my harmonica. I had brought both it and the instruction booklet with me. "To begin playing," said the booklet, "concentrate on blowing and drawing the harmonica using the following chart as a guide. At this point, don't be discouraged if you blow or draw two holes at the same time." Discouraged? I hadn't even put the thing to my lips yet. Harmonicas were distinctly unbeautiful instruments, and if Marylou had wanted to give me something nice she should have chosen a small flute.

"Later in this booklet," said the booklet, "you will learn how to correctly blow and draw pure single tones. For the present, just accept and enjoy the fact that you are able immediately to create a combination of melody and harmony." Utterly discouraged, I put the harmonica back in my pocket and paid the cab driver. As I walked through Dr. Waingloss' lobby I suddenly felt very odd—as though I were shrinking.

The receptionist admitted me at once, and Dr. Waingloss and I stared at each other. His socks did not match and there was a large egg stain on his tie. I wondered if I was going to faint.

"Sit down," said Dr. Waingloss in an unctuous voice. I did so, and then there was a silence.

"How have you been?" he asked kindly.

"OK," I said, gazing at the floor. "How have you been?"

There was no reply.

"That's an interesting garment you're wearing," he said, nodding at my Tappan Zee High School jacket.

"Yeah," I said. And then there was another silence.

Dr. Waingloss cleared his throat, as if he were ready to get down to business. "I thought we might talk about sex roles today."

"Oh," I said. "All right."

"What does the word 'woman' mean to you?" he asked, his pencil stub poised in the air.

"What does it mean to you?" I asked.

Dr. Waingloss ignored my question. "Free-associate. Woman, girl, female, feminine. What comes up?"

"Would you like to hear a dream I had last night?" I asked abruptly.

Dr. Waingloss looked startled. "Why, yes. Go ahead."

I had dreamt nothing the night before, but it had suddenly occurred to me that a bogus dream might keep Dr. Waingloss off my back. And, as Bradley Brown kept telling me, I had a vivid imagination.

"Well," I began, "this dream takes place on Fifth Ave-

28

nue at Christmastime, and I am walking along looking at all the store windows when I realize that someone is walking with me. By my side. And when I turn my head I get a shock, because it is an enormous harmonica."

Dr. Waingloss stopped writing. "A harmonica?"

"Yeah. And it gives me a shock because I have never seen a walking harmonica before. Life-size. And then I get a further shock because it smiles at me and says, 'Do you like Beethoven?' and to be polite I say, 'Yes.' We walk together from Fifty-ninth Street down to the Forty-second Street library and nobody notices us at all. I mean, no one even gives us a glance. 'Well,' says the harmonica, 'this is where I get off. I have a library book overdue.' So we shake hands and I continue down the street—but my heart is beating very fast, like I had just met a movie star or something. And he was only a harmonica."

Dr. Waingloss looked stunned. "Is that the end of the dream?"

"Yes."

"And the harmonica was a male?"

"Definitely. He was wearing a business suit."

"Anything else?"

"I beg your pardon?"

"Was he wearing anything else?"

"I don't think so. But he was carrying a black umbrella."

"I see . . ." said Dr. Waingloss. "Tell me, J.F., have you ever heard the expression 'penis envy'?"

"Well yes," I said. "I think so. Here and there."

29

"And what does this expression mean to you?"

I thought fast, but nothing came to mind. So—for the next fifty minutes—Dr. Waingloss explained all about penis envy while I removed myself mentally and tried not to smell the banana-odor that permeated the room. On Dr. Waingloss' desk was a photo of an elderly woman with bangs that covered her eyes like a sheepdog's.

I lit a cigaret and puffed the smoke into a halo round my head, trying to separate myself from Dr. Waingloss as his terrible words knifed their way towards me. By the end of the session I was enclosed in a kind of nicotine fog, and Dr. Waingloss and I parted vaguely—like two people on a dimly lit street.

Once home again, I locked myself in my room and took out the instruction booklet. "Raise the harmonica to your mouth with one hand at each end," it said. "The forefingers go on top and the thumbs underneath, leaving all the holes open. Now try playing the 8-note scale by following this simple blow and draw chart." Again I felt a sense of despair—as though Doris Villanelle were sitting by my side whispering "*One*-two-three, *one*-two-three." I was no good at taking instructions. Something in me balked.

I thought of Marylou and how much she loved me. I thought of the fact that I would probably die of lung cancer before I was eighteen.

Then I raised the harmonica to my mouth.

The sound that came out was astonishing in its beauty. I could hardly believe my ears, and blew again. Then I drew in instead of blowing out, and produced an entirely different sound. Overwhelmed, I began to blow and draw, blow and draw, moving my mouth up and down the length of the harmonica. I was playing a scale! In the key of C! It was too much.

I began again, moving from the left side of the harmonica up towards the right, blowing and drawing—and then edging my way down towards the left side again. The sound was gorgeous, not esthetic perhaps, but gorgeous all the same. I loved it. The way it reverberated through my head sending slight vibrations down my spine. The way it resembled, ever so faintly, a church organ. I flipped madly through the instruction booklet, looking for a tune to play, and found "Jingle Bells." Instead of notes on a staff it had numbered arrows on a straight line, indicating whether you were supposed to blow or draw. I followed the arrows haltingly and, to my almost unspeakable joy, heard a ragged tune come out of the harmonica. It was—without a doubt—"Jingle Bells."

I raced to the telephone and dialed Marylou's number. "Hello?" she said.

"It's me!" I shouted. "Guess what?"

"Did you just get back from Dr. Waingloss?"

"Yeah, I did. Guess what?"

"How was he this time?" Marylou asked.

"Horrible," I said. "We talked about penis envy. Marylou, listen—I just played 'Jingle Bells' on my harmonica."

A note of cautious joy came into Marylou's voice. "You did?"

"Yeah, I did. And I love it. I love the whole thing. It's

31

so *good*, as Nelson would say. Listen—is he there? Nelson, I mean."

"Yes, he's right by my elbow."

"Would you put him on the phone for a minute? And listen, Marylou, thanks."

There was a pause and then Nelson came to the telephone. "Hello?" he said hesitantly. "This is Nelson speaking."

"Nelson," I said, "this is J.F. How are you?"

There was a wounded silence. "I'm fine," he said.

"Are you really?"

"Yes."

"Well listen, Nelson, I'm calling you to apologize for what I said yesterday. About your being a creep. I didn't mean it."

"You didn't?" he said in a tiny voice.

"No, honestly, I didn't. I can't imagine why I said such a thing, and I want you to forgive me."

"I forgive you," said the tiny voice.

"Are you sure?"

"Yes, I'm sure. I really do forgive you."

A feeling of great warmth and happiness came over me. "Thank you, Nelson. I'm glad we're friends again."

I hung up the phone and gazed at my harmonica, realizing what a lucky person I was. Nelson had forgiven me, and I had the best friend in the world in Marylou, and now I was about to embark on a whole new experience which would stop me from smoking. I would not die of lung cancer before I was eighteen, thus putting an end to some brilliant—if unknown—career, and somehow, someday, I would find the inner strength to withstand the slings and arrows of Dr. Waingloss.

All of which brings me to the saga of Harold Murth.

4

Harold Murth's course was simply named Poetry—and by this we discovered that he meant *all* poetry, ancient and modern, classic and hip. It was very bewildering. One day we would be studying John Milton and the next day Allen Ginsberg. On Monday Matthew Arnold, and on Wednesday Jack Kerouac. Homer kept company with Dylan Thomas, and Christina Rossetti and Sylvia Plath were not incompatible. It was weird.

Palely loitering—his hair paler than his skin, and his clothes of an almost indescribable paleness—Harold would stand at the blackboard gazing at us through his glasses. "There are many voices, but a single muse," he said repeatedly. And every time he said it, I fell asleep.

This, exclusively, had been my reaction to the course—a kind of awful sleeping sickness. The minute we entered Harold's room at 8:45 I would feel my eyelids beginning to droop and enormous yawns would escape me. I sat far in the back, so no one would notice, and sometimes Marylou would sneak out to the faculty lounge and return with a cup of coffee to battle the tides of sleep that were washing over my head. But it was of no avail. Every time Harold said, "There are many voices, but a single muse," or "Poems are the wings of the mind," I would pass out.

I could not stand him. He was so . . . pale. "A fruit," I said to Marylou, "a real fruit." But she, as usual, was compassionate to a fault and decided that Harold had probably been raised by an overprotective mother. At times Marylou sounded like Dr. Waingloss. But what *was* it about Harold Murth? His sand-colored clothes? His thin, pale hair? His watery eyes? The way he would tremble whenever he mentioned a poet named Christopher Smart? I did not know, but he drove me up the wall and if there had ever been a chance of my liking poetry, Harold mutilated it. I did not like any of the poets we studied— not even Allen Ginsberg, who I had once seen walking along 8th Street and who looked like an amiable madman.

"Consider the poet's impulse," said Harold Murth to a class of fifteen pubescent girls. "What it means to be swept up into the emotion of poetry, a need to write so vast that even hunger and deprivation cannot squelch it. Consider the poet's vision, the inner eye that sees not as we see, but beyond—far far beyond."

"I'm going to puke," I whispered to Marylou as we sat in the back of the room.

"Shh," she said.

"Consider also," said Harold Murth, "what it means to reach into the mind's unconscious—that place where all true poetry lies—to plunge into those forbidden areas of fantasy and dream. Consider the risk, the *danger* of plumbing so rich and secret a soil, so private and hallucinatory a landscape."

"I cannot stand this," I whispered to Marylou.

"Shh," she repeated. "It's interesting."

Interesting? I would have sooner studied Slavic Languages with Boris Grotowski—the eighty-year-old Russian who had taught at Miss Howlett's for years and who lived in a tiny room over on the West Side. (And here I must take the opportunity to explain that the curriculum at Miss Howlett's had no connection with the teachers at Miss Howlett's. Or perhaps it was vice versa. The curriculum, indeed, was intensely modern, sporting courses like Mysticism and the Divine, and Crumbling Patterns in the Nuclear Family—while the teachers remained as mid-Victorian as they had been in the 1920's when the school was founded. In addition to Harold and Boris there was simply a clutch of spinsters of varying ages, the youngest of whom, Esther Tilley, looked like an undernourished bird.)

"Poetry," said Harold Murth, "is man's way of conquering death, of defeating those spectres of mortality that haunt and damage the mind. Poetry is, quite simply, man's ladder to God."

And then the bell rang.

"What *I* need is a ladder out of this school," I said to Marylou as we walked down the hall.

"You're very intolerant, J.F."

"Intolerant? The guy's so fruity that you could sell him in the supermarket."

"He is an interesting man," said Marylou. "You're missing the point."

36

"What point? That poetry is man's ladder to God? The whole thing is a fraud."

We parted—Marylou to see her adviser Miss Delacorte, and I to take a harmonica break in the gym. By now I was addicted to the harmonica even more intensely than I had been addicted to cigarets. Three weeks of playing the harmonica and I was a different person. Not calmer, perhaps, but different. It was incredible.

I had quickly progressed from tunes like "Jingle Bells" and "Three Blind Mice" to more complicated—and stirring—pieces like "The Battle Hymn of the Republic." Only yesterday I had learned "Onward, Christian Soldiers," a piece which sounded absolutely inspiring on the harmonica. Where would it all end? With Bach and Beethoven perhaps. For, without being too vain about it, I was an absolutely terrific harmonica player. A natural, as they say. Playing exclusively by ear, I discovered that I did not have to think about the notes of a tune. They simply appeared as I needed them, one by one.

I entered the gym, which was always vacant at this hour of the morning, and sat down on a bench underneath the basketball hoop. I raised the harmonica to my lips and—to my surprise—heard "Molly Malone" issue forth. I had not intended to play "Molly Malone," but it was as good a piece as any other.

I had not smoked for three weeks.

I played "Molly Malone" several times and dovetailed into "Loch Lomond," an equally touching melody. Then my mind returned to Harold. What *was* it about Harold

Murth? His thin, bony frame? His unpolished shoes? The fact that he still wore his class ring from college—a gesture so gauche that I could barely think about it? Why did I hate him? I did not hate Boris Grotowski and he was in many ways much worse than Harold. Boris always smelled of onions, and was known to doze his way through an entire class while his students knitted or read novels. I did not hate Esther Tilley, even though she had embarrassed me terribly last year by getting a crush on me and giving me straight A's in The Crisis of Contemporary Thought—a course for which I had done no homework whatsoever.

(Esther Tilley will appear later in this story, but it should be mentioned that her crush on me was more maternal than erotic. She was always bringing me oranges to eat with my lunch, because she felt I was lacking in vitamin C, and had once given me a book entitled *How to Stop Smoking in Ten Minutes.* She was thin, sallow and delicate—a kind of female equivalent of Harold—and lived with her aunt on 86th Street. They had twelve male cats, all rescued from the streets of New York, and would deprive themselves of necessities in order to buy cat food. Esther Tilley had worn the same winter coat ever since I had entered Miss Howlett's in the seventh grade, but none of the kids thought much about things like that since we all took it for granted that our teachers were supposed to be dedicated and poverty-stricken.)

I finished "Loch Lomond" and went into "The Streets of Laredo"—startling myself with a small trill. Only yesterday I had learned that the people who made my "Marine Band"—the Hohner Company—made other harmonicas as well. Dozens of them. This discovery had almost blown my mind, and I had rushed into a music store and gotten a Hohner catalog at once. It was incredible how many harmonicas Hohner made, instruments with gorgeous names like "Goliath" and "Echo Harp" and "Auto Valve." There was even a harmonica called "El Centenario" which was supposed to be ideal for playing Latin music.

What was it about Harold Murth? His hideous shyness? The way he never looked directly into a student's eyes, but always over her head? His obsession with poets that no one had ever heard of—like Charlotte Mew, a Georgian poet who wrote in the person of a man, wore a bow tie and eventually killed herself? Why did I dislike Harold so much? As yet I had not done a single scrap of homework for his course, and when confronted had decided to say something like, "I'm sorry, Mr. Murth, but people like Charlotte Mew don't really turn me on."

The door of the gym opened and Esther Tilley peeked in. When she saw me, she blushed. "Oh. J.F. I wondered who was in here."

"It's me," I said. "I'm playing the harmonica."

Miss Tilley looked surprised. "Harmonica?"

"Yeah. I've taken it up as a way to stop smoking. Would you like to hear 'Molly Malone'?"

Miss Tilley said that she would love to hear "Molly Malone," and that she was thrilled that I had stopped

39

smoking—so I gave her a small concert on the spot, both of us sitting under the basketball hoop. I tried not to notice that she was gazing at me with adoring eyes. It felt terrible.

Later that day I sat in my room with the door locked, playing "On Top of Old Smoky." Half of me was concentrating on the music and half of me was still thinking about Harold Murth. I had only been in his class for a month, but I was freaking out. Should I go to the principal, Miss Bowker, and ask for a change of venue? Tell Harold that poetry made me faint? Pretend to go insane in the midst of his class? There seemed to be no satisfactory exit except death—and for Harold Murth I was not willing to die.

There was a knock at the door. "Jacqueline? Is that you?"

Who else would it be? I thought. "Yes," I said. "Wait a minute."

I unlocked the door and my mother walked in. "I keep hearing a harmonica in here," she said.

"That's because there *is* a harmonica in here," I said proudly. "It's me. I'm playing the harmonica."

My mother looked at me with an air of faint disgust. "What on earth for?"

Something in me faltered. "I don't know."

My mother sat down at the dressing table and gazed at herself in the mirror. She was wearing a gray wool pants suit and small gold earrings. "That idiot Mabel plucked my eyebrows today," she said. "It was a mistake."

"Your eyebrows look OK."

40

She flashed me a quick glance. "Do you think so? Your father hates it when I pluck them."

"Well, I can't really tell the difference. They look the same, plucked or unplucked."

She regarded herself in the mirror again. "That's because I have eyebrow pencil on, silly." She sighed. "I wonder if *you'll* ever want to wear makeup."

"I don't think so."

She picked up my Swiss Army Knife, contemplated it, and put it down again. "That's what I want to talk to you about, Jacqueline. Your looks."

Inwardly, I groaned. We were about to have the same discussion we had been having for the past four years. "My looks?"

"You know what I'm talking about," she said sharply. "I don't think I can take another year of this. I really don't."

I stared at the floor. "Of what?"

"Of *you*. The way you dress. The clothes you insist on wearing. Do you enjoy making me a laughingstock? Because if you do, you're succeeding."

"I like the way I look," I said in a tiny voice. I sounded like Nelson.

"Well, I don't!" she said, rising to her feet. "You don't look like a boy and you don't look like a girl."

"What do I look like?" I asked.

"A . . . a cab driver!" my mother replied.

I stared at the floor again. "Oh."

"Isn't that psychiatrist doing anything for you? I'm paying him over a hundred a week."

"I don't think he's doing too much."

"Because you won't cooperate!" she said theatrically. "You've never cooperated anywhere! Camp, school, the Girl Scouts. Why must you humiliate me this way?"

She kept on ranting, but I didn't hear her. Because, as usual during these discussions, my ego was deflating like a balloon that had just been ravaged by a pin. It was incredible how quickly my mother could make me feel like a cipher. Sometimes just being in the same room with her would wipe me out. I mean, there she would be, coiffed and enamelled, perfumed and groomed—and there *I* would be, looking like a cab driver. There was not a single thing we had in common, and whenever we went anyplace together both of us suffered—she because she was ashamed of me, and I because I was ashamed of her.

I had a very peculiar dream that night in which my mother and I and Harold Murth were all on an ocean liner together, sharing the same cabin. Then my mother fell overboard and Harold and I were left alone. We walked up and down the deck, discussing Charlotte Mew, and I kept saying what a dumb poet she was and Harold kept saying that I had missed the point. For a moment I considered pushing *him* overboard, but restrained myself, and then Charlotte Mew herself appeared—wearing her men's clothes and looking very neurotic. "Where is this ship heading?" she asked. "What port do we journey to?" I said that we were heading for Zanzibar and Charlotte fainted. "There are lepers on Zanzibar," Harold explained. "We are all lepers," I replied.

And then I woke up.

I pondered this dream for a while, decided not to tell it to Dr. Waingloss, and threw on my Levi's and sweat shirt. As usual, I was going to be late for school. I brushed my teeth, slicked back my hair with cold water, and raced out of the apartment. I took a cab to school, and heard the first bell ring just as I was changing into my uniform in the lockers.

"Damn," I muttered, as I raced up the three floors to Harold's class. I slid into my seat in the back just as the second bell rang. "Close call," I said to Marylou—and she nodded.

Harold conducted his class in what we called the Old Library. This was to distinguish it from the New Library, which was on the second floor and was very modern. The Old Library, on the other hand, had a kind of seedy atmosphere—like a room in an English movie in which a murder is committed. The walls were panelled and the windows were stained glass, and you did not sit at school desks but on chairs of varying comfort and design. Most of the books had been removed, but there were still leather-bound copies of Shakespeare and Dickens, and in one corner stood an old-fashioned Victrola.

To my surprise, Harold was beginning the class with a poem by Charlotte Mew. It seemed like an odd coincidence, and for a moment I felt as if he had read my dream.

"The unenlightened would call this poet saccharine," said Harold Murth. "Or, if you will, corny. But beneath the conventional trappings of her age, Charlotte Mew emerges as a single voice, a cry of despair within a strict and conservative environment. Listen to an early poem:

> *Why do you shrink away, and start and stare?*
> *Life frowns to see you leaning at death's gate—*
> *Not back, but on. Ah! sweet, it is too late:*
> *You cannot cast these kisses from your hair.*
> *Will God's cold breath blow kindly anywhere*
> *Upon such burning gold? Oh! lips worn white*
> *With waiting! Love will blossom in a night*
> *And you shall wake to find the roses there!"*

I cannot say exactly when it happened. Whether it was on the line, "You cannot cast these kisses from your hair," or whether it was, "Oh! lips worn white with waiting!" But somewhere between those two lines a miracle happened. Harold reached out his left hand to emphasize the poem, a ray of sunlight slanted through the stained glass bathing him in gold, and—he looked beautiful. Like a saint. A chill went down my spine and a stab of pain through my head as Harold stood before us bathed in gold, gesturing like some knight in a medieval tapestry, his voice gentle as he spoke Charlotte Mew's words, his eyes an almost translucent blue, his hair gold, the words golden, gold itself spilling from his fingertips, his entire body bathed in gold.

And in that moment I knew—beyond the shadow of a doubt or the slightest supposition—that I had fallen in love.

5

"I can't stand it," I said. "I'll kill myself."

"You will not," said Marylou. "People only do that in novels."

"But I can't stand it. It's driving me mad."

"Then why don't you tell him?"

I looked at her in amazement. "You must be insane."

"Well, how can Harold know you're in love with him if you don't . . ."

"I don't want him to know!" I screamed. "Don't you understand *anything*?"

"Then what is it you want?" Marylou asked helplessly.

"I don't know. To be near him. To find out things about him. I don't know."

Marylou shook her head wearily. She had already explained to me that this was a crush, not love, but I knew differently. It was love—of the most terrible and pervasive kind. The kind that you could die of, or the kind that would last until you were forty. It was love, hideous and gnawing like a toothache. And it would never go away.

"You're such an extremist," Marylou said. "One minute you hate him, and the next minute you're head over heels."

"But don't you see!" I shouted. "My aversion was really attraction! Only I didn't know it."

I sounded like Dr. Waingloss.

"Be that as it may. I feel that you should either tell him or forget the whole thing."

I looked at Marylou in despair. How could she be so dumb? Tell him, and risk the zenith in humiliation? Be made to look like a fool? No. I would never tell him. But I *would* zip into action. "Where's the phone book?" I said.

At that point the door of her room opened and Nelson popped in. "I think it's going to snow," he said cheerfully. "The sky's all gray."

I tried to control myself. "Nelson," I said, "this is October, and it does not snow in October. It is not going to snow."

"I think it is," he said happily. "The sky's all funny and dark."

"Fine," I said. "Great. Why don't you report your findings to the Weather Bureau."

His eyes widened. "Do you think I should?"

"Sure. Call up the Weather Bureau and tell them it's going to snow. They'd appreciate it."

"I will!" said Nelson. "How do I get the number?"

"Ask Information."

"OK!" he said. "That's a neat idea, J.F."

"You shouldn't tease him," said Marylou, when Nelson was gone.

"Tease him? One day I'll kill him. Where's your telephone book?"

46

Marylou handed it to me, and I looked through all the M's until I found the words "Murth, Harold."

It was crazy, but just seeing his name in the Manhattan telephone directory made me tremble. Murth, Harold. A simple name, yet strong. And there was his address. 357 East 94th Street.

"I'm going to stake out his place!" I said suddenly. "I'm going to keep a dossier on him and find out everything."

Marylou looked bewildered. "But why don't you just . . ."

"Because he'd never look at me!" I said, coming to the end of my rope. "He'd never even give me a glance. *God*, Marylou, how can you be so dumb? I mean, when it comes to archaeology and tombs and mummies and things, you're a genius. But about Harold . . ."

"All right," she sighed. "It's all right, J.F. I'll help."

We embraced awkwardly and pulled apart. "Thank you," I said emotionally.

A few minutes later I was in a cab, heading for East 94th Street. To calm myself, I took out my harmonica and played "The Minstrel Boy to the War Is Gone."

"Hey," said the cab driver. "That's pretty good."

"Thank you," I said. For a moment I felt like bowing.

"You a professional or something?" he asked.

"Yeah," I replied. "I'm with a group."

"Rock?"

"No," I said. "Classical. We play Mozart and stuff like that."

"Terrific," he said. "Terrific."

47

I tipped the cab driver fifty cents and stood looking at Harold's apartment building across the street. It was very small and shabby—a brownstone with garbage cans out front and alley cats wandering about. An old lady was leaning out of the window, her arms on a worn pillow. It was terrible.

Tears came into my eyes. Harold Murth was a scholar and a poet, and yet he had to live in a place like this. Why was there no justice in the world? Harold should have lived in a suite at the Plaza on one of the top floors, with a view of Central Park.

I gazed at the windows, wondering which one was his. I thought of him carrying groceries up the stairs. I pictured him late at night, sitting in those barren rooms reading Shakespeare. It was too much.

I withdrew into the doorway of a defunct barber shop, my eyes never leaving Harold's threshold. What had happened to me? Yesterday morning I had simply been J.F. McAllister, and today I was someone else. J.F. McAllister in love. It was weird.

But also beautiful.

I thought back over my life, to the various people who had made their entrances and exits through my heart. Marylou, when we were both twelve. Greta Garbo. Winthrop Honeycomb, my father's best friend, who had once spent a great deal of time at our house. A boy named Pablo Jones, who used to deliver our groceries and was wildly handsome. Had I loved any of these people romantically? Definitely not—with the exception, perhaps, of Greta Garbo.

For a solid year Greta Garbo had pierced my heart with her cold, distant, Scandinavian beauty. I had forced Marylou to attend all of her film festivals, and my memory balks at how many Greenwich Village theatres we sat in watching old prints of *Grand Hotel* and *Ninotchka.* I would rise at three in the morning to watch clandestine replays of *Anna Karenina* on late late television—and nailed a huge poster of Garbo over my bed, a fact which annoyed my mother considerably. I also made a point of hanging around Beekman Place, where Garbo was supposed to live. And then one day I had actually *seen* her, striding down Second Avenue wearing a Napoleonic coat and a man's fur hat. She looked older than I imagined, but beautiful. Cold and distant. Scandinavian. My heart pounding in my breast, I had followed her—no easy thing to do, since Garbo seemed to be the fastest walker in New York—and we had proceeded wildly down Second Avenue, Garbo striding along like a panther and I puffing after her, regretting the fact that I smoked so much. All of a sudden she had turned and confronted me, her face a mask of rage. "Vy are you followink me?" she demanded—and I had been speechless. We stood facing each other for what seemed to be an eternity, and then I had said, "I'm sorry. I thought you were someone else."

But that had been childhood and this was youth. That had been infatuation, while this was love. Please, I said silently, please, dear Harold Murth, come home this minute with your groceries or your laundry. Let me see you enter the building, and take out your door key, and go up the stairs. That is all I want.

But nothing happened.

I stood there until it was dark, and then walked home. I felt both joyful and depressed—no simple combination —and lay awake long into the night, picturing Harold Murth in different circumstances. Harold at the dentist, being brave. Harold at faculty meetings, sighing at the stupidity of it all. Harold reading in the bathtub—that one was hard to picture—and Harold walking languidly through Central Park, a book of poetry under his arm. How could I find out more about him? It was simple. I would rifle his records in the principal's office.

(I have not yet revealed here that there was a side to my character that was less than honest. A side that harbored uncontrollable impulses to rifle people's bureau drawers, and steam open their mail, and go through their coat pockets. A side that wanted to shoplift the way an alcoholic wants to drink. All this was undoubtedly connected to my most recent bad habit of entering a supermarket, taking a huge chocolate bar and eating it while I wheeled an empty basket around—finally departing through the checkout gate with a ten-cent packet of gum. I cannot explain these deficiencies in my character. They were simply *there*, like those mountains that people are compelled to climb.)

The following day I waited until lunchtime, when the principal's office was empty, and then entered it with all the aplomb of a CIA agent about to do a job on foreign soil. Without the slightest fear I proceeded through the personnel files, coming to M—for MacIntosh and Murth—

took out Harold's file, and glanced quickly through it. The news was both thrilling and strange. Harold Murth had been born in Tenafly, New Jersey, attended public schools there, and had finally proceeded to Columbia University where he had received both B.A. and M.A. in English Literature. He had worked for an electronics firm for five years and was now writing his Ph.D. thesis. This was his first teaching job.

I left the principal's office quickly and hurried down to my locker, where I had a brand-new notebook with a marbled cover. I sat down on a bench and recorded my knowledge thus far.

Name *Murth, Harold.*
Age *30.*
Place of Birth *Tenafly, New Jersey.*
Education *B.A. and M.A. from Columbia University.*
Work Experience *Electronics. Teaching.*
Habits

I paused, my pen in midair. I did not know his habits. Nor did I know what he did on weekends, if his parents were alive, or what hobbies and recreations he pursued. There were a million things I did not know, and I was a person who *had* to know things. Dr. Waingloss said that this came from a severe anxiety-neurosis, but I felt that it came from simple curiosity.

Harold had looked so beautiful in class that morning. So . . . ethereal. Why had I never noticed that he had long,

51

tapering Renaissance fingers? Or that his hair, though sparse, was the color of spun flax? Why had I never listened, really listened, to his voice—which resembled a Shakespearean actor's? Why had I been so blind? For delicacy, purity, and intellect Harold had no rivals. He was alone among men.

He had been telling us about Gordon Bottomley—another poet I had never heard of—who had once written a play called *King Lear's Wife.* It seemed an odd title, but no matter. Harold's memory was inexhaustible. He knew the names of more obscure poets than were filed away in the 42nd Street library. Suddenly I vowed to become an expert on obscure poets—thus startling Harold one day with something like, "By the way, Mr. Murth, I've been reading the works of Polly Chase Boyden, and it seems to me . . ." or, "Mr. Murth, I've just looked into the work of a man named Orrik Johns, and I wonder if you would mind . . ."

Harold's clarion voice brought me out of this reverie.

"And thus we become aware of the ancient—one might even say atavistic—connection between drama and verse, between ritual and civilization. Bottomley's pull was in both directions, yet his poems were an integral part of his plays, and his plays, perhaps, gave deeper credence to his poems. It is not the form one chooses but the impetus behind it—the thrust of necessity, the poet's necessity, the necessity of art."

I had no idea what he meant, but loved every word. How incredible that he had had to work for an electronics

52

firm and now lived in a shabby brownstone. Was this the fate of scholars and poets? It was. The more beautiful a person's soul, the more he had to suffer in this world. And it was wrong, wrong, wrong.

The bell rang—and after one last loving look at Harold, I sprinted downstairs to the library, about to become the world's expert on obscure poets. And indeed, the very first book I laid my hands on had a plethora of them. Hazel Hall. Wilfred Wilson Gibson. Helen Hoyt. Fenton Johnson. Aline Kilmer. Agnes Lee. Maurice Lesemann . . . I was overwhelmed. There were more obscure poets than one could have hoped for. I would never run out.

Where was Harold at this moment? In the bathroom? The faculty lounge? Smoking his pipe on the little balcony that adjoined the teachers' dining room? Suddenly, and without even trying, I saw the whole *gestalt* of Harold Murth. It was as if his pipe, the shabby tweeds he wore, his pale hair and unpolished shoes, his golden voice and genius-mind had all merged together in a single flash of meaning. I saw him. I knew him. And what I knew was wonderful. He was the yin to my yang, the light to my darkness, the rain in the aridity of my desert. We belonged together—only he did not know it.

Elated, I raced through the rest of the morning and left school at lunchtime to go out and buy a new harmonica. The harmonica's name was "Goliath."

6

"Think of it this way," said Dr. Waingloss. "There are three tapes going round in your mind simultaneously and these tapes are called The Child, The Parent and The Adult. The Child and The Parent have been programmed, but The Adult we can change."

Fraud! said my inner voice. Last week you were talking about Behaviorism and today it's Transactional Analysis. Fraud! Phony! Charlatan!

But of course I said none of this aloud. Instead, I looked as bland as possible and tried to ignore Dr. Waingloss' rumpled hair and dirty shirt-cuffs. He looked worse today than usual, as though he had been through a tiny war. The picture on his desk—that of an elderly woman with bangs like a sheepdog's—was turned directly towards him, and at moments I had the odd impression that he was addressing the picture instead of me.

The reason I knew that we had leapt from Behaviorism into Transactional Analysis was because my reading program in psychology was now rivalled only by my reading program in obscure poets. To defend myself against Dr. Waingloss I had gone to the library and come home with a huge pile of books with titles like *You and Your Gestalt*;

Death—The Ultimate Transaction; and *Interpersonal Madness*. These had served to arm me against the horrors that Dr. Waingloss perpetrated upon me twice a week. I had also bought a book of Freudian dreams, and was now able to supply Dr. Waingloss with at least one dream per session. These phantoms of the mind dealt exclusively with umbrellas, bananas, cigars and frankfurters and seemed to please him very much.

"So let us talk about *your* Child and what is on his tape," Dr. Waingloss said gently. "Let us see what we can find out about him."

"Her," I corrected. And then there was a pause. "Do you have any kids?" I asked.

Dr. Waingloss' face went rigid. "Why do you ask that, J.F.?"

"Just curious."

"What comes up about kids? What surfaces?"

"I don't know, really. I was just wondering if you were married."

He gave me a sharp glance. "Would it bother you if I was?"

"No!" I almost screamed. Then, calming down, I tried another approach. "Do you like kids, Dr. Waingloss?"

He smiled like a snake about to swallow a rabbit. "Would I be seeing you if I didn't?"

Sure, said my inner voice. To collect a buck you'd be seeing Dracula.

"Let me tell you my latest dream," I said, hoping to divert him from the tape inside my head who was really a Child. "It's about this banana who hates his father. . . ."

Dr. Waingloss drooped a little as I plagiarized a dream from one of Dr. Freud's more spectacular patients. In the end, the banana turns into an ape and devours both parents.

I finished the dream and Dr. Waingloss looked blank. And tired. And rather old. Suddenly I felt sorry for him.

"Look," I said, "why don't you tell me something about yourself? We'd have more fun that way."

"Fun?" said Dr. Waingloss.

And then I realized that he had never had fun in his life. "Sure," I said. "Why not?"

"I would like to return," he said stiffly, "to the tape inside your head whose data has not yet been programmed."

And so we returned to that tape, and by the end of the session I was in a very foul mood. I left without saying good-bye and was just making my way through the reception room when I stopped cold in my tracks. There, sitting demurely on a couch, was a patient of Dr. Waingloss' that I had never seen before. By now I was thoroughly familiar with the patient who preceded me, a woman I called The Dragon Lady—and the patient who came after me, a man I had named The Mad Scientist. But this patient was new. And not only was she new, she was just my age. And beautiful. Stunning. Chic. I came to a halt and looked at her. Long blond hair. Bell-bottoms. Turtleneck sweater made out of cashmere. Boots. And then—like an avalanche of sour dreams—all the reasons I was seeing Dr.

56

Waingloss came down on my head. I was seeing him because I was a sixteen-year-old girl who looked like a cab driver. Because I was not socially acceptable. Because my mother was ashamed of me.

I stared at the new patient and she stared back. To my horror, I knew that I was going to cry. So, with a loud clearing of my throat, I proceeded out of the building and across the street into Central Park. I sat down on a bench, trembling a little, and took out Goliath—my new harmonica.

It was a comfort to look at him in his neat green box, and after calming down I raised him to my lips. An absolutely majestic sound issued forth because Goliath was an echo harp. In other words, he provided his own tremolo. I played "Down by the Sally Gardens" and "The Ash Grove" and felt better. An old lady walking a bulldog smiled at me.

I tried to decide how many people in the world approved of my looks—but only came up with Marylou and her mother. And possibly Esther Tilley. But Esther Tilley was unreliable because her subconscious mind had confused me with a teen-age boy and gotten a crush on me. Esther Tilley would not have given me a tumble if I looked like a teen-age girl. As for the rest of the world—parents, relatives, teachers, doormen and salesladies—none of them approved. It was as if my passage through life were secure as long as I did not open my mouth. Until that moment I got away with being a teen-age cab driver. But the minute I said, "Excuse me, do you have the time?" or,

"How much is that pair of skates in the window?" the whole world, it seemed, turned and stared at me aghast. A girl's voice in the body of a boy! A boy's outfit disguising the body of a girl! Horrors.

I went into my World War I medley—"Over There" and "It's a Long Way to Tipperary"—and was quite surprised when the old lady with the bulldog sat down beside me. She was wearing a shabby black coat and a tiny hat.

"Lovely," she said of the music. "Lovely."

"Thank you," I said.

"You play so well," she murmured.

"Thank you," I said again.

" 'It's a Long Way to Tipperary' . . ." she mused. "The boys at the front sing that all the time, don't they?"

"I don't know," I said. "Do they?"

"Yes," she said. "They do. My nephew is with General Pershing. He drives an ambulance."

"In Vietnam?"

She gazed at me. "In France, dear, France. Are you making some special effort for the war? Are you knitting?"

For Vietnam? I wanted to say again. But something told me that we were not on the same wavelength.

"I don't think so," I said. "I mean, I was in a demonstration once, but that's all."

"It's the shell-shock I worry about," she said sadly. "So many of the boys come home vague and confused."

"From where?" I asked.

"France," she murmured. "France."

The bulldog was sitting between us like a referee—

58

turning his head from one to the other. I had a strong desire to leave.

"Well," I said. "I have to go now."

The old lady looked disappointed. "Do you, dear? What a pity. But promise me you will knit something this month. We must all do our part."

"Sure," I said. "Right." And then I got the hell out of there.

By the time I got home I felt suicidal—so I locked myself in my room and took out my Harold Murth dossier. In the past ten days I had seen Harold go into his building three times and come out twice. Thus, I had gleaned the following information.

Name *Murth, Harold.*
Age *30.*
Place of Birth *Tenafly, New Jersey.*
Education *B.A. and M.A. from Columbia University.*
Work Experience *Electronics. Teaching.*
Habits *Comes home at approx. 5:00* P.M. *Carries* The New York Times *and a bag of groceries. Has usually misplaced his door key.*
Laundry *Dong Ho's. 94th Street.*
Entertainments *Seemingly, none.*

It was a lean record, I had to admit. But standing in the doorway of a defunct barber shop was not the best way to plumb a person's soul. What I needed to do was tail Harold on foot. Find out where he spent his time, if he attended the movies, if he had any friends. Marylou was helping me observe him at Miss Howlett's, but his behavior there was circumspect. When not teaching, he sat in the library correcting papers, or smoked his pipe on the balcony off the dining room. He did not converse with the other teachers, and rarely smiled. Watching him in class I wanted to cry out, "Harold, Harold, smile! The world is not such a terrible place!"

Why was Harold Murth so sad? What had turned him into an introvert? I saw a probable background for him— a life of physical deprivation and mental wealth. He had undoubtedly grown up in one of the poorer parts of Tenafly, struggled through school as a shy, brilliant, insecure student—and been tortured by his peers. Instead of going out for varsity football, Harold had read John Donne. Instead of dating and drinking beer, he had sat in the public library writing sonnets. To add to his misery, his mother was unaffectionate and his father drank. Perhaps, at some early age, an older woman had tried to seduce him, thus placing in his mind a fear of the opposite sex. "Why can't you be like other kids?" his no-good, drunken father would chide him. "Why are you a sissy?" But manhood, for Harold Murth, had consisted of the Renaissance values of poetry, music and art, and by the age of eighteen he had escaped to Columbia University and a scholar's education.

And then he had had a breakdown.

I was sure of it. After struggling to receive his M.A. Harold had lost faith. In life, in art, in poetry. Thus he had gone to work in an electronics firm. Bitterness had set in, and cynicism. He had drunk a bit too much and dated shady women. But then somehow—I had not yet worked this out—his faith in art had returned and he had come to teach at Miss Howlett's and write his Ph.D. thesis.

Did I fit into his life? The answer was—distressingly— both yes and no. Yes, in the sense that Harold needed someone to look after him, to protect him from the world while he wrote his thesis and meditated on art. No, in the sense that I was not good enough for him, smart enough for him, or attractive enough for him. The truth of the matter was that I was not attractive at all.

I lay down on my bed and stifled a groan. What had begun as a joyous experience was now turning into something painful beyond description. I was sixteen and he was thirty. I was gauche and crude while he spoke and moved like Hamlet. Indeed, he *was* Hamlet—a man caught in a spiral of inaction, a person who saw, all too tragically, the sad devices of this world.

Groaning over the hopelessness of my life, I slept.

I woke the next day in a better frame of mind—determined to stake out Harold's building and see what I could learn. Marylou had reported to me that Harold never took buses, that he walked everywhere, and this accounted for his late arrival at home every afternoon. Sure enough, at 5:00 he strode up to his house—as I crouched in the barber shop doorway—and fumbled for his door key. He looked beautiful and weary, his arms filled with packages, and I had to restrain myself from rushing across the street and taking his bundles. For a moment it crossed my mind that he might be tubercular, but I banished the thought. He was not tubercular, he was just . . . esthetic. A modern-day Hamlet living on 94th Street. A poet who had to fight his way through the contemporary swamp of supermarkets and dry-cleaning stores. With all my heart, I wished to take these burdens from him.

Harold's door key seemed to be deeply lost. Putting down his groceries, he went through all his pockets. This gesture was unbearably touching because it made him look like a little boy. Eventually he found the key, picked up his packages again, opened the main door of the building and vanished inside. I put my hands to my cheeks and found them flushed. How wonderful he was.

I stood there for a few minutes, reluctant to go home and reluctant to stay. I thought of Harold putting his groceries away and having, perhaps, a small glass of red wine. Did he watch television at night? I doubted it. He read. He studied. He wrote.

I was just about to leave when I saw an oddly-familiar figure approach Harold's building, pause on the front step, take out a key and go inside. In what seemed to be a mental time-lapse of a hundred years my mind came to the slow conclusion that this had been—and indeed was—Esther Tilley.

7

"Miss Tilley," I said, "would you care to have a cup of coffee with me after school?"

Esther Tilley blushed. I had never invited her anywhere before, and it was evident that she was both startled and pleased.

"Why, yes," she said. "Yes, indeed."

"Good," I said. "Meet me in front of the building at three fifteen. I'll take you to Schrafft's."

My *savoir-faire* was not real, of course, but manufactured. Ever since I had seen Miss Tilley enter Harold's building I had been 1) filled with rage 2) filled with despair 3) filled with curiosity. Was it possible that they were lovers? My wildest stretch of imagination could not get them both into one bed—but you never knew. People were strange. *I*, as a matter of fact, was strange because the very idea that Esther Tilley might prefer Harold to me was driving me wild. Which was weird, since I didn't even like her.

I tried to picture Esther Tilley naked, but failed. And as for Harold, I couldn't even get his jacket off. They were, most definitely, two people who should not be naked. But were they . . . Could they . . . The thought was maddening.

At 3:15 Miss Tilley and I joined company in front of the school, and after a courtly little bow, I took her arm and led her down Madison Avenue. I was wearing chinos and sneakers and my Tappan Zee High School jacket—and it was obvious that Miss Tilley was excited by our assignation. Perhaps I had not lost my charm after all.

Once in Schrafft's I took her coat, hung it up, and then —just as I was sitting down—had a brainstorm. I would get her drunk.

"Miss Tilley," I said, "let me buy you a glass of sherry. It's very raw out."

"Why, no it isn't," she said. "The weather is fine."

"Let me buy you a glass of sherry anyway. It will help you relax."

I glanced at the waitress. "The lady will have two sherries, very dry, and I will have two chocolate sodas."

"Two?" said Miss Tilley.

"I always order two of things," I lied. "It saves having to reorder."

"But . . ."

"It's because I have a compulsive personality. No control."

Miss Tilley smiled shyly. "You mustn't say that about yourself, J.F."

"It's true," I said. "Did you know I was in therapy?" Miss Tilley looked shocked. "Whatever for?"

"Anxiety-neurosis. I'm seeing a very famous man over on Seventieth Street. We haven't even scratched the surface yet."

"Of what?"

"Me," I sighed. "I have a very rough home life, you know."

Miss Tilley leaned across the table and touched my arm. "No, J.F., I didn't know. I'm sorry."

"It's OK," I said. "Everyone has a burden to bear."

At that moment the waitress brought our drinks. I watched Miss Tilley take a sip of sherry. "Is it all right?" I asked. "Dry enough?"

"Lovely," said Miss Tilley. "This is really very sweet of you, J.F."

"That's OK," I said. "I've wanted to take you out for a long time."

To my satisfaction, Esther Tilley blushed.

I watched her take another sip of sherry, wondering how long it would take to get her drunk. "I have some unusual courses this year," I said casually. "Like Contemporary China and Mr. Murth's poetry course."

I observed her to see whether Harold's name would produce a reaction. It didn't.

"I think that's marvelous," she said. "You know, J.F., you do so well when you apply yourself. So wonderfully."

"I know. But this neurosis I have seems to *keep* me from applying myself. That's why I'm in therapy."

Esther Tilley took another sip of her drink—a bigger sip. "I don't think you have a neurosis at all. I think you're very well-balanced."

"Thank you," I said. "You know, the course on China, with Miss Harper, is pretty good—but Mr.

Murth's poetry course beats everything."

"In what sense?" she asked, taking another sip of sherry.

"In the sense that it's so . . . unconventional. We read everybody. The Greeks right through Allen Ginsberg."

To my satisfaction, I saw that she had almost finished her first glass of sherry. She drank faster than I thought.

"I have always thought," said Miss Tilley slowly, "that you had a very unusual mind. For a girl."

"In what sense?" I asked.

She paused. "In the sense that you do not seem weighted down by conventionality."

"Is that good?"

Miss Tilley hiccuped and quickly raised her napkin to her mouth. "Yes, J.F., I think it is. You must not quote me on that, however."

"I won't."

She stared at me—then glanced quickly away. "This is very kind of you, J.F. To invite me to Schrafft's."

"It's nothing," I said. "Have you ever sat in on Mr. Murth's course? I think you'd like it."

"I'm sure I would," she said, beginning her second glass of wine. "I'm typing his thesis, you know."

"You're what!" I yelled, blowing my cool entirely. "What did you say you were doing?"

"Typing his thesis," Miss Tilley replied. "I delivered the first half of it to him yesterday."

Inwardly, I groaned with relief. How incredible life was.

"How come?" I said. "How come you're doing that?"

"Well . . ." Miss Tilley began. And then I realized that she was beginning to get high.

"It's this way," she said, leaning across the table confidingly. "Mr. Murth is living in rather straitened circumstances at the moment, and since I have an electric machine I offered to help him out. In other words, he can't afford a professional typist."

Can't afford a typist? my inner voice screamed. Why didn't he come to me? I would have hired a whole typing school.

"I don't understand," I said.

Miss Tilley touched my arm again. "You promise not to mention any of this. I mean . . ."

"Of course I promise. I just don't understand the situation."

"It's a long story," Miss Tilley sighed, her hand still on my arm.

"I'd be interested to hear it."

"Well . . ." she began, pausing to take another sip of sherry. "Harold is a brilliant scholar, but he seems to have been plagued by poverty most of his life. He worked his way through college, I believe, and is the sole support of an ailing mother in New Jersey. My impression is that he has been saving money to go to England to complete his thesis—but I doubt that he will ever get there. And the paper can't be completed in America."

"Why not?" I said. "Why can't it be completed? What's the problem?"

"The thesis is called *Madness and Redemption in the*

Poems of Christopher Smart—but the documents that Harold needs to complete it are in Cambridge."

"Gee. And he doesn't have the money to go there?"

"I'm afraid not," said Miss Tilley.

"Gee," I said again. And then I noticed that Miss Tilley had finished her second glass of sherry. "Have some more sherry," I suggested.

Miss Tilley giggled. "Oh, no. I couldn't do that."

"Sure you could. It's cold outside. Another sherry!" I called to the waitress.

After that things got very strange. Miss Tilley had a third glass of sherry, and a fourth, and the afternoon waxed and waned. I switched from chocolate sodas to coffee—and was very tempted to smoke, but didn't. The more Miss Tilley drank, the more she giggled and touched my arm. And the more she did these things, the more uncomfortable I became. Finally, around 5:30, I helped her into her coat and we staggered out of Schrafft's. She was very drunk.

"So nice," she muttered, as I helped her along Madison Avenue. "So nice of you."

"That's OK," I said nervously. "Let's find a cab."

I hailed a cab and helped her inside, and we proceeded uptown. By now Miss Tilley had slumped against me like a modest sack of potatoes, and I was feeling very nervous. I had meant to get her drunk, but not *this* drunk.

"So kind of you," she kept muttering.

"That's OK," I said. "It's OK. Everything is going to be OK." I wondered how her aunt was going to feel about her coming home plastered.

68

"Here we are," I said as the cab drew up in front of her building.

"So nice," she muttered. "So very kind."

I thrust a bill at the driver and helped Miss Tilley onto the sidewalk. I felt terrible about the whole situation.

"Would you like me to come upstairs with you?" I asked, thinking of her aunt.

"No, no," she said. "Certainly not. No, no, no."

"You're sure?"

"Oh, yes. Sure."

"Well, then," I said. "Good night."

She gazed at me emotionally. "You are a wonderful girl, J.F. You have a wonderful mind."

"Thank you," I said.

Tears came into Miss Tilley's eyes. "May I kiss you good night?"

God, I thought, what have I done? "Of course," I said bravely. "Go ahead."

Miss Tilley reached up and kissed my cheek. "Good night, J.F."

"Good night," I said. "Good night."

She staggered into the building and I stood there—feeling like a crumb. As a matter of fact, I had never in my life felt crummier, meaner, or more awful. So I headed back to Madison Avenue where there was a florist who stayed open until seven.

Using the last of my allowance, I sent Esther Tilley six roses.

8

Harold Murth was a pauper. He had worked his way through college. He was the sole support of an ailing mother, and could not afford to go to England. The one thing he cared about—his thesis—would remain unfinished, gathering dust in some shabby bureau drawer.

Angrily, I brushed the tears away and washed my face. The school bathroom was filled with noisy girls combing, preening, putting on makeup—and none of them had a care in the world. None of them was in love the way I was in love, and thus none of them suffered. Harold Murth was a pauper, and there was no one on this earth to help him.

That morning, in class, I had stared at him with such intense devotion that he had noticed it and glanced nervously away. He had never looked more beautiful—his eyes a translucent blue, his hair falling slightly over his forehead. And his voice had sounded like Laurence Olivier's as he said, "Neither success nor failure can touch the artist's creation once he has completed it. A work of art is its own voice, its own justification, and is not affected by criticism or neglect. The act of creation has been the artist's *raison d'être*, and what follows afterward is up to fate, to the gods of chance."

But the gods of chance were not smiling on Harold Murth, and there was no one to help him. He had come into this world alone and would depart alone, unaided and unloved. There was no one to help him through graduate school, to buy him little luxuries, to pay his dental bills, to take him to England.

No one but me.

I straightened up and stared at myself in the mirror. The shrieks and giggles of the girls around me faded like a dream. *I* would help Harold. I would send him to England and support his invalid mother. I, J.F. McAllister.

Once I had decided this, a kind of burden fell from my shoulders. Granted, it was a large task—but I felt capable of fulfilling it. How terrible that my allowance had been cut recently. How terrible that my inheritance from various relatives was years away. *Nevertheless.* I would send Harold Murth to England.

Marylou tugged at my arm. "J.F.? Are you coming with me to get Nelson?"

"No," I said, "I'm going to follow Harold this afternoon."

"Oh." She looked slightly hurt. "We haven't done anything together for days."

"I know," I said apologetically. "I'll come over tonight. We'll talk."

She brightened a little. "OK. You look tired, J.F. Have you been sleeping?"

"Not very well. It's this thing with Harold."

"I understand," she said. And the moment she said it,

71

I knew that she *did* understand. Her blindness about Harold had given way at last to a kind of weary comprehension.

I stationed myself in front of the school, and at 3:30 Harold came out and lit his pipe. Then he walked over to Madison and headed uptown. I trailed half a block behind, my heart pounding. This was the first time I had actually followed him.

We were approaching November now and the day was chilly, but Harold wore no coat. He probably doesn't own a winter coat, I thought bitterly. He's probably never had a winter coat in his life. I thought of myself—of my sock collection and Danish ski sweaters. I thought of my archery set and ten-speed bicycle, the dozens of presents I always got for Christmas, my large allowance. I felt ashamed.

(On the other hand, my allowance had recently been cut—and the background to this is worth going into. A week before I had fallen in love with Harold I had been bumming around Fifth Avenue and 46th Street and, on impulse, had decided to go over to Abercrombie & Fitch. It was one of my favorite stores since it featured items like safari outfits, tents, and golf carts. Once inside the store, I had browsed happily about, admiring electric back massagers, aluminum tennis rackets, miniature TV sets and oil portraits of lions and tigers. I was wearing my Down With Reality sweat shirt, faded Levi's, and old sneakers. I felt pretty good until I realized that a detective was trailing me, watching carefully as I picked up items, looked at them and put them down again. I knew he was a detective because all New York department-store detectives wear hats.

We proceeded around the first floor—I picking up items and looking at them, and the detective trailing behind. I was getting angrier and angrier because this detective was judging me solely on my looks. Not my brains, or my character, or my education, but my goddamn *looks*. And then something in me snapped. Pausing in front of a counter, I said to a salesman, "How much is that canoe?"

"I beg your pardon?" said the salesman.

"There is a small canoe behind you," I said. "How much is it?"

"Ah," said the salesman. "The canoe. It's three hundred dollars—on sale."

"I'll buy it," I said.

The salesman looked startled. "Very good, sir. I mean, madam. Do you wish to take it or have it sent?"

For a moment I almost laughed. But the salesman was serious. "Charge and send," I said, producing my mother's charge plate. And then, turning to the detective, I said pleasantly, "Handsome canoe, don't you think? I'm taking it up to my fishing lodge in Canada."

He blushed crimson. "Indeed, madam. I hope you enjoy it."

So there I was, the owner of a canoe—and the more I thought about it, the more nervous I became. My mother had loaned me her charge plate in order to purchase a sweater and some socks. Not a canoe. What would she say about this? I soon learned the following week, when the canoe was delivered. First, she told the delivery man that it must be a mistake. Second, when she discovered that it was not a mistake, she turned slightly gray. Third, when I confessed what I had done, she became hysterical. "Where am I going to paddle a canoe!" she screamed. "Into the Plaza? What am I going to *do* with this thing?" Eventually we sent the canoe to a relative who had a place in Maine, but as a result of this caper my allowance was docked and an evening curfew imposed. My father, I believe, found the whole thing rather amusing, but since I saw so little of him I was never sure. And this, to make a long story short, is why I was at present feeling financially depleted.)

Harold paused in front of a bookstore, looked intently into the window and went inside. I loitered on the outside, watching every motion he made. Puffing on his pipe, he drifted over to a rack of paperbacks that said POETRY and stood there browsing through recent titles. He made no move to buy a book, however, and this cut me to the heart. You, I said to myself, can bum around New York buying anything you want. *Harold* cannot even purchase a paperback copy of Yeats.

Harold stayed in the bookstore for twenty minutes. Then he came out and proceeded uptown again. I kept my distance from him, noticing, with love, how gracefully he walked—what good posture he had. Next he went into a grocery store and purchased a frozen dinner, a bottle of skimmed milk, and some yogurt. Then he turned east and headed home. I did not feel foolish following him. Instead, I felt as though I were protecting him, as though silent waves of love were emanating from my mind to his. I loved Harold Murth and was going to send him to Cambridge to complete his thesis. I would protect and cherish him for the rest of my life.

But how could I send him to Cambridge on my allowance? I was not permitted to touch my savings—which were considerable because of birthday gifts from generous people like Winthrop Honeycomb—and the stocks that had been purchased in my name were in my father's keeping. I had no way of earning money, and was not yet up to stealing it. For one desperate moment I saw myself holding up a bank, Marylou and Nelson by my side, all of us wearing face-masks and clutching rifles, but the image faded.

Harold stopped in front of his building, looking for his key, and I—as usual—crouched in the barber-shop doorway across the street. He found the key at last, picked up his groceries and went inside. I felt as abandoned as an orphan. The doorway of his home separated us like a continent and there was no way for me to get inside. If Harold had possessed a fire escape I would have climbed it gladly and peered in at him. But his building had none.

Disheartened, I decided to walk down Lexington Avenue to the Melody Music Store, which had a fairly good stock of harmonicas. By now I owned three—Marine Band, Goliath, and Echo. The latter was my favorite, a rather small harmonica of modern design, and I carried him everywhere along with my Swiss Army Knife. I practiced Echo in between classes at school, at lunch hour, and —to my mother's annoyance—in the middle of the night. I played him lying in the bathtub, sitting up in bed, and walking along the street.

It was amazing how proficient I had become—graduating from folk songs into simple classical pieces like Ravel's "Pavane for a Dead Princess." Once, spurred on by the radio, I had even played a tiny chunk of a Brandenburg Concerto. I was playing single notes now, as well as chords, and was seriously thinking of looking in the *Times'* classified ads for an instructor. Perhaps this was to be my future—classical harmonica in Carnegie Hall. Or, at the other end of the spectrum, perhaps I would merely wind up playing with an all-girl band in the Middle West.

As a child people had asked me, What do you want to be when you grow up? and I had always replied, "A policeman. A fireman." No, no, they had protested—only little *boys* become firemen and policemen. So out of spite I had switched to professions like telephone operator, nursery school teacher, waitress and salesgirl. The truth of the matter was that I had no bloody idea what I wanted to be. Nor did I know what I would major in at Vassar in two years. Providing they accepted me, of course.

Suddenly I decided that if anyone asked me what I was going to major in at Vassar, I would reply, "Sex Therapy." That would shut them up.

I had reached 86th and Lexington and was just about to cross the street when I noticed two boys in Levi's and

76

sweaters standing on the corner. They had long hair and serious faces—and oddly enough they were playing violins. A crowd was standing around them and at their feet was an open violin case with a sign in it that said

WE ARE MUSIC STUDENTS. PLEASE HELP US
CONTINUE OUR EDUCATION.

I noticed that there were quite a few dollar bills in the violin case, and even a five.

I drew closer and listened. The boys were playing something that sounded like a Bach concerto, and it was terrific. People were enthralled. And when they came to the end of the piece, everyone burst into applause. It was great. I put fifty cents into their violin case and continued down the street, past a bakery, a shoe store, a pet shop and a florist.

And then it hit me.

I had found the way to send Harold Murth to England.

9

"There's a sale on at Saks," said my mother. "Fake furs."

"Oh?" I said politely.

"Do you think I should get one?"

"Sure," I said, my mind light-years away.

It was Sunday morning and we were having brunch together—my mother wearing a pale blue dressing gown, and me wearing my Steve McQueen outfit. My father was in Chicago, on a business trip.

"Do you like me in brown or black?" she asked.

"I don't know," I replied. "Either."

"Well, you must have a preference," she said. And then, all of a sudden, she got angry. For no reason at all.

"I'm tired of shopping! What's the point of trying to look attractive when your father's never home?"

"I don't know," I said. "What *is* the point?"

"It's a wonder I haven't drunk myself to death these past years," she said—a remark that seemed irrelevant, because she didn't drink.

"Why don't you take a lover?" I suggested. But the minute I said it, I knew I had made a mistake. Her eyes became the size of saucers.

"What did you say, Jacqueline?"

"Uh . . . nothing. Nothing, really."

She stared at me. "I sometimes wonder if you are in your right mind. Isn't that school doing anything for you? You are going to the best school in New York."

"I know," I said.

"And Dr. Waingloss. What about Dr. Waingloss?"

"What about him?"

"Oh, you're impossible!" she said irritably. "You refuse to communicate."

I refuse, I thought. *Me?* Wild, man. Absolutely wild. I rose to my feet. "Well, I think I'll go now."

My mother looked at me suspiciously. "Where?"

"To the Metropolitan Museum—with Marylou. There's an exhibition of tapestries."

"Since when have you been interested in tapestries?"

I tried to look innocent. "Oh, for a long time now. I just never mentioned it."

My mother sighed. Suddenly she looked tired. "Well, don't stay too long. Maybe we'll go to a movie later."

I was—very briefly—touched. "OK, Mom. That would be nice."

"Have a good time," she said, as I made for the front door.

"Thanks," I called back.

I took my bicycle out of the basement and pedalled down Park Avenue. I was not, of course, going to the museum at all—but to Central Park to make my debut as a street musician. Marylou was bringing a sign, and an old hat of her father's, and we were about to embark on my new career. Being a paragon of virtue, Marylou had objected strenuously for a solid week—interpreting the whole thing as a rip-off. But eventually she had given in and I loved her for it. Marylou was a neat human being.

She was waiting for me at the end of the Mall, and after chaining my bike to a tree, we arranged my things. First we put the hat on the ground with a few quarters in it, and then we set up the sign Marylou had carefully lettered. It said

I AM A MUSIC STUDENT. PLEASE HELP ME CONTINUE MY EDUCATION.

"Wow, am I nervous," I said to her.

"You have nothing to be nervous about," she said sternly. "You play very well."

"But I feel like I'm opening on Broadway or something. My heart is going a mile a minute."

"Nonsense," said Marylou, sounding like a maiden aunt. "Begin."

She stepped a few feet away and waited expectantly. Almost paralyzed with fear, I raised Echo to my lips and started to play a song from *Fiddler on the Roof.* After that, I intended to play pieces from *My Fair Lady* and *Gypsy.* Light entertainment.

It didn't sound too bad. Marylou stood watching me as though she were a passerby, and pretty soon two women wheeling baby carriages came to a halt. Then a man walking his dog stopped to listen, and three old ladies. Suddenly I had a small crowd.

Right on cue, Marylou stepped forward and put a dollar into the hat. Almost immediately, one of the old ladies did the same. Then the man with the dog put in fifty cents, and the younger women each put in a quarter. My heart soared.

I was really playing well now—oblivious of everything but the music. I finished my Musical Comedy medley and dovetailed into my cycle of English Folk Songs. I felt great. And Echo had never sounded better. His tones were brilliant and clear.

Maybe I really *am* a musician, I thought, sailing into "Down by the Sally Gardens." Maybe this is what I am meant to do with my life.

I finished "Down by the Sally Gardens" and was startled to hear a scattering of applause.

"Where do you study, dear?" asked one of the old ladies.

"Study?" I said. "Ah . . . Juilliard. I'm in my first year."

"Lovely," she said. "Absolutely lovely."

There were about twenty people standing around now, so I whipped into my American medley—"The Streets Of Laredo," "Shenandoah," and "Oh, Susanna." For a really smashing climax I ended with "The Battle Hymn of the Republic." Then everyone applauded and I took a bow. The hat was filled with dollar bills.

"This is unbelievable," I said to Marylou.

"Keep playing," she said under her breath. "You're marvelous."

Two hours later we sat in the cafeteria at the Zoo, drinking Cokes. I had taken in seventeen dollars.

"It's wild," I said to Marylou. "I mean, people were throwing money into the hat as if there was no tomorrow."

"It's the way you look," she explained.

"How do you mean?"

"Well," she said, "you look so . . . shabby, if you'll forgive the word. Like an orphan or something."

I took a long sip of my Coke. "Do you still disapprove of this?"

She looked over my head and sighed. "Yes, I do. But I don't know how else you're going to raise the money. Have you figured out how long it's going to take?"

"Well," I said slowly, "I don't know. I want to raise at least a thousand, and if I could make twenty bucks a day that would be . . ."

"Fifty days."

"Right. Only I probably couldn't make twenty every single day. Considering rain and everything."

"I would suggest," she said, "that you work the theatre district."

"Huh?"

"Work the theatre district at night, at intermission time. People who go to the theatre in New York are usually from out of town. They have money to spend."

"No kidding," I said.

"You could say you were doing homework over at my house." And then Marylou looked very sad. The situation wasn't sitting well with her at all.

"Look," I said, "I know how moral you are and everything—and I know how this gig depresses you. But the money isn't for me. It's for Harold."

"I'll be glad when it's over."

"It's funny," I said. "I don't know whether I will be or not. I mean, standing up in front of all those people today—it felt nice."

She smiled. "You're just a ham at heart, J.F. That's why I love you."

I lay in bed that night arranging my schedule. In the first place I had school every day, and in the second place I had my reading program. Obscure poets for Harold, and psychology for Dr. Waingloss. I would have to practice Echo a good deal—adding tunes to my repertoire—and in addition to all this there was my Harold Murth dossier, which I expanded every afternoon. *Then* there was my research into the life of Christopher Smart—who had turned out to be an eighteenth-century poet who went insane—and at night I would be working the theatre district with the harmonica. This schedule seemed to leave no time for 1) sleep 2) homework 3) social life. But what the hell. I had once heard my father say that the key to success was organization, and I believed him.

The Harold Murth dossier had grown by leaps and bounds, accruing small interesting items such as the fact that Harold possessed exactly one suit and two tweed jackets, that his pipe tobacco was called "Valiant," and that he brought his own lunch to school every day. He did not take buses or cabs and—to my delight—jogged on Saturday mornings. I had discovered this quite by accident, arriving in the barber-shop doorway one Saturday to see Harold sprint out of his house in a T-shirt and pair of shorts. Thrilled, I had jogged after him, across First, Second, and Third Avenues, towards the park. Then, to my great annoyance, I had lost him in the middle of a Hungarian parade—all the participants dressed in national costumes, and the sidewalks on Fifth Avenue jammed with viewers.

I knew other things about him as well. The fact that he ate health foods and carried a bottle of vitamin C in his pocket. The fact that he was desperately uncomfortable around women, using a kind of Edwardian courtesy to evade them. "My dear Miss Harper," he would say, brushing swiftly past her in the hall. "Lovely weather," he would mumble to Miss Reed, opening a door for her and then heading in the opposite direction. Only Boris Grotowski made him feel comfortable, and the two of them could often be seen on the school's fourth-floor balcony, smoking and chatting.

Harold conducted his poetry course in a way that was unusual for our school. In other words, he lectured. Other teachers were always saying, "And what do *you* think of that concept, J.F.?" but Harold rarely asked anything of anyone. Instead, he stared above our heads and rambled on—in his beautiful voice—about obscure poets like Merrill Moore, Jessica Nelson North, and Elder Olson. At times, I felt that he did not know we were there—that he was addressing some vast audience of the soul. Or perhaps addressing himself. I was certain now, beyond the shadow

84

of a doubt, that he wrote poetry. Why else would he go on and on about the poet's mission in life? About the thrust of necessity? The thrust of art? I wondered if he had been published, but somehow doubted it. Harold's poetry would be too beautiful for the modern world. We lived, I had decided, in an age of ugliness, an era in which people were drinking and smoking themselves to death, in which love meant sex and sex was ridiculous. An era in which politicians were not only corrupt, but unattractive. An era in which the arms race was more important than the human race.

Only Harold Murth was pure. And with that thought glittering in my mind like a star, I slept.

10

I stared at Dr. Waingloss—trying to analyze him. Perhaps there was a *reason* for his untidy clothes and rumpled hair. Perhaps there was a long string that unravelled back into his childhood, and at the end of that string was the answer. An overly-strict father? A fussy, neurotic mother? God, I thought, I am beginning to think just like him. Dr. Waingloss had a reason for everything.

For example, Dr. Waingloss and I had recently been plumbing the reasons I wasn't gay—my life-style so clearly indicating that I should be—and I had happened to ask him why people were gay in the first place. As though someone had pushed a button in his head he had rattled off, "The cause of homosexuality is a rejecting father and an overly intimate mother." Then the recording had switched off and he had sat looking at me. How weird that it should be so simple, I thought. And then I had thought, OK, what about gay orphans? Or people raised on an Israeli kibbutz? What about gay Arabs—gay natives in darkest Africa? All of them couldn't have had a rejecting father and an overly intimate mother. What about gay sheep and gay cows? Dr. Waingloss, you are a fraud.

Today he was discussing my Transference to him—

which was really a laugh, since I didn't have any. But what the hell, I thought. If Dr. Waingloss wants to think I am transferring, let him think it. Poor man. He looked especially tired and the banana-smell in the room was so strong that I was amazed we were both sitting upright. I kept staring at the picture on Dr. Waingloss' desk—the one of an elderly woman with bangs like a sheepdog's. His mother? Aunt? Wife? Last week, when I had entered the room, he had been polishing the picture with Windex and a paper towel.

"What has happened here," said Dr. Waingloss, "is that you have transferred on to me the feelings you have had for some significant male in your past. Most likely, your father."

Brilliant, I said to myself. The only trouble is that my past has had no significant males.

Dr. Waingloss seemed to be talking to himself. "The therapist is simply an empty slate upon which the patient writes the story of his life. Do you understand?"

What I understand, said my inner voice, is that this room smells of bananas and that I am going to be sick.

I had a strong desire to change the subject. "Do you think it's going to snow?" I asked.

"What comes up about snow?" Dr. Waingloss replied. "What surfaces?"

"Nothing surfaces," I said. "I just wondered what you thought about the weather."

"What are *your* feelings about the weather?" Dr. Waingloss said gently.

"I don't have any feelings about the weather."

"But it was you who brought the subject up."

"Well, I don't think the weather is a subject," I said testily. "I mean, weather is simply weather."

"Do you ever dream about snow?" he asked.

Oh damn, I thought. "Sure," I replied, "all the time. Only last week I dreamt about a snowflake who thought he was God."

And so I spent the next twenty minutes making up a story about a snowflake who had intimations of divinity —and then the session was over. Despondent, I walked down Central Park West. Dr. Waingloss charged sixty dollars an hour and here we were talking about the weather. What a cheat. I looked at the darkening sky and decided that it probably *would* snow, and that immediately made me wonder whether I could work 47th Street that night. In the past two weeks I had been working the theatre district on Thursday, Friday, and Saturday nights —and Fifth Avenue on Monday, Tuesday, and Wednesday afternoons. On Sundays I worked the park, so the whole thing was pretty well organized.

It was surprising how much company I had. On Fifth Avenue and 48th there was a hippie named Krishna who sold jewelry and was always on the lookout for cops—and on 51st Street, near Saint Patrick's Cathedral, there was a fat pretzel seller named Benny Goldstein who thought I was a boy and called me "son." Farther up Fifth Avenue was a crazy-looking woman who sold terrible paintings and talked to all the passersby—and the theatre district, of course, was rampant with kids like myself who played musical instruments. The only difference being that they were legitimate.

Outside of the cold weather, I liked being a street person very much. The competition was tough, but I secretly felt that I had an edge over the other peddlers and musicians and this was—as Marylou had pointed out—my looks. The androgyny I had suffered from all my life was a huge advantage on the street, since people felt that they were either giving money to 1) a rather delicate young boy who played the harmonica 2) a brave and stalwart young girl who was working her way through music school. I couldn't lose, and was already averaging twenty dollars a day—all of which went into my Harold Murth bank account.

I had decided that the thing I loved most about Harold Murth was his strength. It was not a conventional kind of strength, nor was it even very masculine. But there was a streak in his character—well documented in my Harold Murth dossier—that seemed to me to be indomitable, dauntless and brave. Granted that he had the appearance and manners of a poet. Granted that he was very shy and seemed not to like women. Nevertheless. I sensed in him a manliness that was very Greek, or if you will, androgynous.

I must stop using the word "androgynous" I thought, as I hailed a cab.

I settled back against the worn leather seat and watched Central Park whiz by as we crossed town. I now had a photograph of Harold and was eager to put it up on my wall. I had taken it with my Polaroid yesterday as Harold came out of school, and though it was rather blurred and showed only his back, nevertheless it was *him*.

I was just entering the apartment when I heard my phone ringing—so I sprinted into my room to answer it. It was Marylou.

"How was your session?" she asked.

"Brilliant," I replied. "We talked about snow."

"Oh. Listen, are you going to work the theatre district tonight?"

"Sure. It's Thursday."

"Well, maybe you could give it up—just this one time. My mother has invited us to a play-reading."

"No kidding. Whose play?"

"Hers. The one she wrote last year called *Shovel.*"

"Is that the one about the big machine that digs up a whole town?"

"Right. They're having a backers' reading of it tonight at Melvin Babb's."

"Who's he?" I asked.

Marylou sighed. It was obvious that I should have heard of Melvin Babb. "He's a very famous director, J.F. He's directed Tennessee Williams and everyone."

"Oh. Sorry."

"So if you want to come, be here at eight o'clock and we'll go over with my mother."

"OK," I said. "Great."

Promptly at 8:00 I arrived at the Browns', and was startled to see that both Marylou and Bradley Brown were dressed up. Long skirts and everything. I was simply

90

wearing sneakers, jeans, and my Tappan Zee High School jacket.

"I'm sorry I didn't dress up," I said.

"Nonsense," said Bradley Brown. "You look fine."

Which was the beautiful thing about Bradley Brown— she always accepted people as they were.

Once we had found a cab she took out her lipstick and compact and worked on her face a little bit. "I'm terribly nervous," she said. "Some important people are going to be there."

"How much money do you have to raise?" I asked.

"Seventy-five thousand. And that's only *off*-Broadway. The backers are friends of Melvin's."

"And he's going to direct?"

"Right. It's a miracle, really. He's very much in demand."

Melvin Babb's apartment building was on the East River, and very posh. A doorman took our names and phoned them upstairs. Then we went up in the elevator. Melvin Babb himself was waiting for us on the threshold and he gave me rather a shock. He was only about five foot three and very fat. Also, he was wearing a Chinese robe.

"Darling," he said to Bradley Brown. "You look absolutely divine."

"Well, I'm nervous as a cat," she replied. "I hope you don't mind, Melvin, but I brought Marylou along. And her friend, J.F."

Melvin Babb looked at me appreciatively. "Oh," he said, "sweet. Very sweet."

"How do you do?" I said.

91

We entered the apartment and I got another shock. There were plants and antiques all over the place, and pieces of stage sets, and paintings and statues and mirrors and paperweights and photographs of famous people. Two tropical birds were flying around loose, and built into the wall was a fish tank with purple fish in it. It was really a weird place. I didn't like it at all.

Melvin collapsed on one of the oversized sofas. "You're the first to arrive," he said, "and I'm *already* exhausted. These readings take the very soul out of me."

A maid in uniform came up to me and asked what I wanted to drink. I ordered a Coke.

"*God*," said Melvin Babb, "the brutality of it all. There are times when I just want to move to Southampton and forget the whole thing."

"What whole thing?" I asked.

He sighed. "The theatre, my pet, the theatre. The whole thing's become so terribly brutal. There are nights when I cry myself to sleep."

"Gee," I said, "that's too bad."

"Where did you *get* this creature?" Melvin asked Bradley Brown. I assumed he was referring to me. "She's divine."

By now we all had drinks—Cokes for Marylou and me, and white wine for Melvin and Mrs. Brown.

Melvin Babb put a cigaret into a long ivory holder and lit it. "Did you see the new Hackett play?" he asked Bradley Brown.

"Not yet," she replied.

"Well, it can be easily missed. *So* pretentious, my dear. It's all about cannibalism and incest, and as I said to Roger, after *Suddenly Last Summer* what could one possibly say about cannibalism that would be relevant? Williams has said it all. Do you know the play?" he asked me.

"Not really," I said. "Not well enough to quote."

"*Sweet,*" Melvin said to Bradley Brown. "Absolutely adorable. Where did you get her?"

A tropical bird zoomed over my head and landed on the arm of my chair. It made me very nervous.

"What I love about *your* play," said Melvin to Mrs. Brown, "are the textures. The crude and the delicate intertwined. And the rhythms, my dear. So subtle. So Chekhovian."

"You're very kind," said Bradley Brown.

"No," he sighed, "I am not kind. But I do have my little flair."

"For what?" I inquired.

"For *mise-en-scène*," said Melvin, patting my hand. "A small thing, but mine own."

And then, a million people started to arrive.

The variety was amazing. There were people in evening clothes and people in blue jeans. People with beards and elderly dowagers with little dogs. It was the oddest assortment I had ever seen, and after perusing them for a while I decided that most of them were phonies. Someone began to tend bar and the maid passed smoked oysters and pink sandwiches. The food, I decided, was weird.

And then Harold Murth walked in.

"God!" I said, choking on a sandwich. "Oh, my God."

"What is it?" asked Marylou. "What's wrong?"

"Look who just walked in the door."

"Ohhh," she said under her breath.

"What on earth is he doing here, Marylou?"

"I don't know," she said calmly. "But I hope you'll make the most of it."

11

Harold Murth did not notice me. Everyone got drinks and sat down, and the actors started to read—but Harold didn't notice me at all. There was a look on his face of mingled shyness and concentration, and while the actors read he simply stared out the window at the East River.

As for me, I was a wreck and couldn't concentrate on anything. What was Harold Murth doing here? Why had he come? Was he a secret playwright? A friend of Melvin Babb's? A moonlighting actor? The possibilities were endless. Meanwhile, the play droned on and on and people sipped their drinks or stepped quietly over to the bar for fresh ones. In my nervousness I ate a dozen sandwiches and drank four Cokes.

As far as I could make out, Mrs. Brown's play was about a small town which is being terrorized by a huge mechanical shovel. The shovel keeps digging houses up and throwing them away, and no one is willing to do anything about it because they are all intimidated. Since no one wants to antagonize the shovel, it eventually digs up the entire town and then moves onward. At the end of the play the only person left is an old man, and he sits amid the ruins muttering, "How did it happen? How did it all happen?"

Suddenly the play was over and people were applauding. To my horror, Harold moved towards the door. "He's leaving!" I whispered to Marylou. "What should I do?"

"Go after him," she said.

"Go after him! But I couldn't. I can't. I . . ."

"It's now or never," said Marylou.

So I edged towards the door, but unfortunately got caught up in a little swirl of people who were trying to get to the bar. After endless seconds of saying, "Excuse me. I'm so sorry," to the human eddy I was trapped in, I reached the elevator. Harold was nowhere to be seen. Panic-stricken, I decided to descend by foot and raced down the stairs to the street. Harold was half a block away, heading west.

"Mr. Murth!" I called. "Mr. Murth!"

He turned in surprise as I galloped up to him. It was obvious that he didn't recognize me at all.

"It's me," I said. "J.F. McAllister."

"J.F.?" he said.

"I guess you don't recognize me out of uniform. The school uniform, I mean."

A look of recognition passed over his face. "Oh. Miss McAllister. Forgive me."

"I was at the play-reading," I said breathlessly, "and I saw you there. It was nice, wasn't it? So contemporary and everything. So modern. Mrs. Brown is a friend of mine. I really dig her plays. And Marylou is in your class. Marylou Brown."

It occurred to me that I was talking too much.

"Yes," said Harold. And then there was a pause.

"I think I'm going your way," I said with false cheerfulness. "I mean, why don't we share a cab or something? I live near you and we could share a cab."

Harold looked embarrassed. "I had intended to walk."

"OK," I said. "Great. I mean, why don't we walk together? I live right near you."

He gave me a look that was tinged with pain. "You do?"

"Yeah. I do."

"Excellent," he said.

We started off together, at a rapid pace, and I offered up a little prayer of gratitude that I wasn't smoking. I could never have kept up with him if I was. "Beautiful evening," I said, trying to make conversation.

"Yes," he said. And then we were silent.

I glanced at Harold by my side, at his fair hair and lean body, and felt a shudder go down my spine. We had never been this close to one another before. The fact that he was taller than I was thrilled me. The fact that he could walk faster. The fact that, with quiet braveness, he wore no overcoat. He was an incredible man—esthetic yet virile. Sensitive while being self-sufficient.

"Terrific weather," I said.

"Yes," he replied. "It is."

"No pollution. I mean, you can see the stars and everything."

"Yes," he said.

I was beginning to get the message that he wasn't exactly thrilled to be with me. On the other hand, when would an opportunity like this occur again? Years, *decades* might pass before I would bump into him again socially, and I simply had to make the most of it. Please, I prayed to the God with whom I perpetually made bargains, please let him invite me up to his apartment. If you let him invite me up to his apartment, I will stop shoplifting and reading other people's mail. I will no longer go through my mother's bureau drawers and my father's overcoat pockets. I will never again swipe another giant Hershey bar.

All of a sudden we were standing in front of Harold's building on 94th Street. My heart began to pound like a drum. "Well," I said gaily, "here we are."

"Yes," said Harold Murth.

"Didn't take us long, did it?"

"No," said Harold.

He is not going to invite you in, I told myself. This is your one big chance and you are about to blow it. I stared at him for a minute. "Mr. Murth?"

"Yes?"

"Mr. Murth," I said firmly, "I am feeling sort of faint. So I wonder if you would invite me in for a cup of coffee."

All the color seemed to drain from his face. "I beg your pardon?"

"A cup of coffee," I said. "I need a cup of coffee."

"I'm very sorry—but I have no coffee in the house. I don't drink coffee."

"Well then, what about tea?"

"Tea," he repeated.

"Yeah," I said. "A cup of tea would do just as well."

"Fine," he said.

He looks like he is being taken to the gas chamber, I told myself. He doesn't want you to come in. He doesn't even like you. What have you done?

We proceeded up the dingy staircase, Harold in the lead, and by the time we reached the fifth floor I really did feel faint. The halls of his building were filthy and there was a strong smell of cooking in the air.

"Here we are," he said stiffly.

"Great," I said.

His apartment gave me a terrible shock—because there was nothing in it. Nothing. In the living room was simply a small bookcase of books, one chair, and a tiny table. Beyond the living room was a bedroom with a cot in it, and a minuscule bathroom. The kitchen, which resembled a closet, was in the hall. The place was immaculately clean, but empty. The only ornament was a large engraving of Christopher Smart on the wall.

"Nice place," I said.

"Thank you," he replied. And then he vanished into the kitchen.

I sat on the one chair and studied the living room again. It was true. All Harold owned were a few dozen books, a portrait of Christopher Smart, a single chair and a table. It was amazing.

He returned to the living room holding a cracked white mug. "Your tea, Miss McAllister."

I rose clumsily to my feet. "Oh, thanks. Thanks a lot."

"Do sit down," he suggested. So I sat down again.

I tasted the tea—which had neither cream nor sugar in it—and winced.

"That is herb tea," he explained.

"Oh," I said. "No kidding."

"Coffee," he announced, "is decidedly acid. Hard on the stomach."

"I see," I said, taking another sip of the herb mixture. It was terrible.

I had never felt so uncomfortable in my life, so I stood up again. "Wouldn't you like to sit down?" I said.

"Certainly not," Harold replied. "The chair is for you."

"Oh," I said. "Thank you."

Harold stood there, watching me drink the tea, and the longer he watched me the harder it became to drink it. I felt desperate, anxiety-ridden, doomed. It was time, I decided, to bring up an obscure poet.

"I've been reading the works of Humbert Wolfe," I said casually. "Are you familiar with him?"

Harold looked faintly surprised. "Why, yes. I used to own a first edition of the *London Sonnets.*"

It was the most personal thing he had said all evening. I felt encouraged.

"No kidding," I said. "They must have been pretty valuable. I mean, he's really an interesting man. His use of imperfect rhyme, for example."

Harold averted his eyes. "Indeed. His rhyming schemes were very original."

"And the fact that he was in the civil service. That part really kills me."

100

"How so?"

I searched my mind. "Well . . . it's such a weird combination. Poetry and the civil service. Not too many people could hack it."

Harold gazed over my head. "It's true. The strain of it, I fear, shortened his life."

A terrible silence descended on us.

"Nice picture of Christopher Smart," I said, nodding at the wall.

"Thank you," he said.

And then there was nothing left to say. Absolutely nothing. I felt like a fighter pilot who has failed his first mission and is about to be drummed out of the squadron.

(The metaphor is a poor one. Actually, I felt like crying. For here were the two of us, me and Harold Murth, and there wasn't a thing I could do to get close to him. I could not fling myself at his feet, utter words of love, weep, faint, scream, kiss, or hug him. I could not tell him what was in my heart because 1) he would not have believed it 2) he would not have cared. As a matter of fact, gazing at him that evening, sitting there on his one miserable chair with silent words of love galloping through my mind, it occurred to me—just for a second—that my enterprise was doomed. Harold Murth was a totally self-sufficient person. He was shy, withdrawn, and independent. He did not like people, women especially, and had no interests other than his work. The thousand dollars I was raising to send him to England was not enough to entice him out of his shell. He was, without a doubt, the most composed, aloof, introverted, and brilliant person I had ever met.)

101

Harold glanced at his watch. "I'm afraid it's getting rather late."

I jumped to my feet, spilling the tea. "Right. I'd better go."

"I hate to be rude," he said, staring at the wall, "but my bedtime has long passed."

"Absolutely," I said, moving towards the door. "Thank you for the tea."

"You are entirely welcome," he murmured.

I stopped in my tracks. "There's just one thing. . . ."

"Yes?"

"Well, if you don't mind my asking, what brought you to Melvin Babb's house tonight? I mean, are you a theatre-nut or something?"

I could have bitten my tongue. "Theatre-nut" was a very poor expression.

"Melvin Babb is my cousin," Harold said quietly. "He invited me."

"Oh," I said. "I see."

But I did not see at all—and as the cold November air bit my cheeks and I walked home in the starry darkness, I felt a despair so profound that I thought that I would die. You're going to die, I told myself. You're going to die of love.

No, you're not, said another—smaller—voice. You're going to go on playing the harmonica.

12

I was talking to Benny Goldstein, the pretzel seller who worked in front of Saint Patrick's.

"So what I sez to him is this," said Benny. " 'You stay on your side of the street and I'll stay on mine.' Like, it's a free country. Right?"

"Right," I said shivering. It was a cold day.

"Live and let live is my motto," said Benny, "but not that guy. Oh, no. You know what he sez to me? He sez, 'You don't own Fifth Avenue, man. So get the hell out of here.' "

"And then what happened?" I asked.

"Nothin'," said Benny. "Nothin' happened. Which was fortunate 'cause I would have punched him in the nose for two cents. You think I was wrong? You think I should have handled it some other way?"

"Nope," I said. "I think you did the right thing."

Benny Goldstein was talking about a hippie named George, who sold leather belts and was trying to muscle in on the territory around Saint Patrick's. All of us on Fifth Avenue, as a matter of fact, were a little worried about George because he had a very big operation. Two tables with handmade leather belts on them, and a striped umbrella when it rained.

"Operators," said Benny Goldstein, "the world is fulla operators. Wise guys."

"Right," I said.

"You take some of these bums, they ain't done a day's work in their lives. Handmade leather belts! They was probably made in Japan."

"Right," I said. I was getting a little tired.

"I ain't got nothin' against the hippies," said Benny. "I mean, they gotta survive like anyone else. But they don't show no respect. You could be old enough to be their grandfather and there's no kind of respect."

I nodded.

"So if you want my advice, son, you stay away from that creep. Play your mouth organ and have a good time. Kids should have a good time."

It was no use explaining to Benny Goldstein that 1) I was not a boy 2) I was not playing the harmonica as a lark, but to make money. It was, as a matter of fact, useless to try and explain anything to Benny Goldstein at all. The best one could do was stand and listen to his diatribes against hippies and drug addicts, the welfare state and Mayor Lindsay. On the other hand, Benny always gave me free pretzels and steaming cups of coffee from his thermos, so, despite the one-sided nature of our relationship, I liked him quite a lot.

By now I had come to think of myself as a bona fide street person—someone who knew how to rake in the money and avoid the cops. And, most particularly, someone who knew how to avoid my mother. I was always on the lookout for her, as though her coiffed hair and mink coat were about to slide around the corner at any moment. But I had not glimpsed her once. Nor had I glimpsed Tippy Bernhardt, Marylou's parents, or my father—who sometimes darted uptown at cocktail time to imbibe with friends. I was averaging twenty dollars a day and felt that in terms of finance God was on my side.

As for the rest of my psyche, it was troubled. My encounter with Harold, ten days ago, had disturbed me so deeply that I could barely concentrate. To me, our proximity that night had been as thrilling as a collision between Orpheus and Eurydice. To Harold, it had obviously meant nothing. Passing me in the school corridor the next day he had simply nodded and hurried onward—as he did with everyone. Seeing me in class he had merely gazed over my head and rambled on, in his beautiful voice, about the fact that poets are the unacknowledged legislators of the world. Finally we had collided in the school library one afternoon—both of us veering around a stack of books at the same time—and once again I had tried to grab opportunity by the tail. "Mr. Murth?" I said loudly.

He looked at me through his glasses as though he had never seen me before. "Yes?"

"It's me, Mr. Murth. J.F. McAllister. I'm in your poetry class. At 8:45. In the mornings."

Harold frowned. "Ah, yes. Miss McAllister."

"I wanted to thank you for the cup of tea."

"Tea?" he repeated.

I felt like weeping. "You gave me a cup of tea the other night. In your apartment."

"Oh. But of course," said Harold.

105

"Well . . . I just wanted to thank you."

"You are entirely welcome," he said, reaching for a volume of T.S. Eliot.

And that was the end of the encounter.

"He doesn't know I'm alive!" I said to Marylou the following day. "I'm going to kill myself."

"But what do you *want* from him?" she asked, her patience worn thin by this endless topic.

"I want . . ." I said. And then there was a cataclysmic pause. "I want to marry him."

We stared at each other—for the truth had surfaced at last. Granted, it was as much a shock to me as it was to her, but the words had sprung from the depths of my subconscious, and there was no denying that I meant them. I wanted to marry Harold and change my name to J.F. Murth. I wanted to be with him for the rest of my life.

Marylou looked alarmed. We were sitting on her bed with the door locked against Nelson, and it seemed as though all the color had drained from her face.

"You can't be serious, J.F."

I gazed at her. "I am completely serious."

"But what about college? What about your life?"

"There is no life for me without Harold. He is the only thing I want."

(And indeed, what had I ever wanted before? An archery set? A ten-speed bicycle? Suddenly, sitting there with Marylou, I felt as if I had just stepped over an invisible line—the line that separates children from adults. For the first time in my life I wanted something real and was willing to sacrifice for it. For the first time in my life I knew the meaning of the word commitment.)

Marylou faltered. "Would it help you to . . . have an affair with him?"

I could tell what this suggestion had cost her. Marylou was so moral.

"No," I said firmly, "it would not help at all. Besides, I doubt very much if Harold is the type of person who has affairs. I want to marry him."

"But why!" she almost shouted.

The words came of themselves, without my having to think of them. "Because, Marylou, there are no two people on this earth righter for each other than me and Harold. And if we miss each other now, there will never be another chance. Don't you see? There *aren't* any more Harold Murths. He is the only one I will ever find."

A tear glittered in Marylou's eye. "I don't know what to say, J.F. You've changed so much. This whole experience has made you . . . older."

It was true, I thought, as I stood on the street corner listening to Benny Goldstein. I was turning into a different human being. I, who had never had a goal in my life, now had one. I, who had been completely selfish and spoiled, wanted nothing more than to make Harold Murth happy. But how to do it? How to reach him? Harold was as distant as an ice maiden. He positively glittered with remoteness.

"Society boy," Benny Goldstein was saying of Mayor Lindsay. "Movie star. What does he know about running

107

a city? You get one of your garbage strikes, one of your power failures, and this joker goes off to the Bahamas for a sunburn. Big shot."

I nodded absently, my feet numb from the cold. It was finally occurring to me that in order to marry Harold Murth I was going to have to be more aggressive. Following him home from school and keeping a private dossier on him were not enough. What I had to do was make him notice me. Bring my existence into his consciousness in a way that was both dramatic and permanent.

Bidding Benny Goldstein farewell, I turned on my heel and headed for the nearest florist shop. I would send Harold a plant for his apartment. God knows, it was bare enough. And after that, I would send him a gift-basket of fruit. I would keep forcing my way into his mind until he could not ignore me.

At the florist's, which was on Park Avenue, I picked out a huge pot of yellow chrysanthemums and wrote Harold's name and address on the tag. Then I enclosed a card which said, "With best wishes for the winter season. J.F. McAllister." The whole thing cost twelve bucks, and I sent up a little prayer of gratitude that my allowance had been reinstated. The salesman was giving me a fishy look because of my clothes, but I stared him down. "I would like this plant delivered at five thirty this afternoon," I said in my best Miss Howlett's voice. "Do you charge for delivery?"

"Oh no, madam. Indeed not," said the salesman.

"Very good," I said. "Thank you so much."

"Thank *you*, madam," said the salesman, opening the door for me.

I stepped out onto Park Avenue, elated. There was no end to the things I could send Harold, all with my name attached. Food from Charles & Co. Records from the Liberty Music Store. Volumes of obscure poetry from the Gotham Book Mart. Coffee mugs from Jensen's. Gift certificates from Hammacher Schlemmer.

As far as Harold Murth was concerned, New York was about to become a winter festival.

13

"And thus," said Harold Murth, "we have seen how the work of poets like Grace Fallow Norton easily prefigure Edna St. Vincent Millay, sounding a trumpet call, if you will, for that kind of lyric sadness that was to become so fashionable in the 1920's. When Norton writes, 'World, world, I could have danced for thee/And I had tales and minstrelsy,' we receive a strong hint of what was to come later. Norton was not so much an innovator as a bellwether, but she helped to change the poetic conscience of her time."

And then the bell rang.

Girls scattered everywhere, hurrying to the next class, and I was just heading out the door myself when Harold said, "Miss McAllister?"

I paused in midflight. "Yes, Mr. Murth?"

Harold cleared his throat. "May I talk with you for a moment?"

My heart began to pound wildly. "Of course," I said.

I walked over to Harold's desk and stood there, my arms full of books. He gazed over my head. "Miss McAllister . . ."

"Yes?" I said. "Yes?"

"I received . . ." said Harold.

"Yes?" I said encouragingly.

"I received a . . . plant yesterday," he concluded.

"You did?"

"Yes," he said, "I did. Actually, it was more of a . . . pot. A pot of chrysanthemums."

"No kidding."

Harold averted his eyes, as though from a terrible accident. "The card bore your name."

"No kidding," I said again. "Well, I guess that's because it was from me. The pot, I mean. I sent it."

"You did?"

"Yeah," I said boldly. "I did."

A look of pain crossed Harold's face. "I see. Well, I felt that I should say thank you. It was very kind."

It's nothing, I felt like saying. Think nothing of it, because today you are going to receive a basket of fruit from Charles & Co. and tomorrow you are going to get a gift certificate from Scribner's bookstore. All of which is destroying my allowance, but what the hell. I want you to live a little.

"I'm glad you enjoyed it," I said.

"I did enjoy it," he replied, gazing into the air. "It was very attractive."

"Did you water it?"

Harold looked startled. "I beg your pardon?"

"I just wondered if you watered it. It should be watered."

"Of course. How stupid of me. I shall water it this afternoon."

"Great," I said. And then there was one of those si-

111

lences with which my life seems to be afflicted.

"Well," I said with false gaiety, "I have to run now. I'll be late for French."

"Indeed," he said, and turned back to the blackboard.

A few minutes later I sat in Mlle. Etienne's class, reliving the encounter. Had Harold been pleased by the plant? Yes and no. Actually, he had been more startled than anything else, since it was all too evident that no one ever sent him presents. A wave of sadness swept over me as I tried to imagine what it would be like never to receive presents. Thank God Christmas was coming. For Christmas I would *drown* him in gifts.

Mlle. Etienne was absorbed in reading us an essay on the French Revolution, in French, so I took out my Harold Murth bankbook. I was nowhere near the thousand-dollar mark, a pinnacle I had hoped to reach by the 25th of December. On the constantly-lit stage of my mind was the ultimate scene in which I showed up, unannounced, at Harold's apartment and presented him with the check. He would of course protest, go pale, demur. But I would insist that the money had been raised in the name of scholarship and Christopher Smart, not for the personal devices of Harold Murth. He was to think of the thousand dollars as a grant, a fellowship, a contribution to the world of letters. He was to quit his job at Miss Howlett's and purchase a ticket for England. I had not yet worked out the scene in which I accompanied him to England, because this part was difficult to project. Would we get married before or after the trip? What would I tell my parents? And what about Marylou? Marylou and I had not been parted a day in our lives since we were twelve, and I was not entirely sure what a separation would do to her mental health.

I replaced the bankbook in my briefcase and took out Echo, my favorite harmonica. For one wild moment I had an impulse to play the "Marseillaise" right in the middle of Mlle. Etienne's essay on the Revolution—but refrained. I had become so advanced in my musical technique that I was now "bending" notes, using trills and glissandi, and employing dozens of methods learned from my library of instruction booklets. Though Echo was undoubtedly my favorite, because he was in the utilitarian key of C, I also owned harmonicas in the keys of G, A, and E. The next step in upward mobility would be to purchase a chromatic harmonica, since this wondrous instrument allowed you to play sharps and flats by simply pressing a lever at the side.

Later that day I sat in Dr. Waingloss' office, listening to him talk about Archetypes and the Collective Unconscious—half of my mind on his spurious explanation of Jung, and the other half on Harold. I pictured Harold and me on the plane to England. Harold and me strolling the English moors. Harold and me standing in Saint Paul's Cathedral, listening to the heavenly sound of a boys' choir. It was odd, but I had not yet pictured Harold and me making love. Every time my mind touched on the topic, it skidded away.

(To say, at this point in the story, that I was a virgin would be an understatement. I was not just a virgin, I was

113

a monk. A nun. A contemplative. One of those angels in religious paintings who never have parts. I was, as a matter of fact, so sexually unawakened as to be almost a neuter. Dutifully, and with great patience, I had read all the sex manuals of the day—books that described 204 basic lovemaking positions, books that recommended having sex in bathtubs and closets, books that told suburban housewives how to get jobs in massage parlors. I had attended pornographic movies—where you *can* get in if you are under eighteen—and had sat there in a state of remote shock, as though I were witnessing open-heart surgery. Nevertheless. I was still as innocent as a kitten. And Marylou, if possible, was even more innocent than that. If sold into White Slavery, the two of us would have been a total loss.)

"There are two systems in the unconscious," Dr. Waingloss said somberly, "the personal, which is made up of repressed events in an individual's life—and the Archetypes, or inherited tendencies, which form the Collective Unconscious. It is important that we distinguish between them."

"Could we open a window?" I said.

"A window?" said Dr. Waingloss. "Why?"

"Because," I said with rare honesty, "it smells of bananas in here."

Without a comment, Dr. Waingloss went over to the window and opened it a crack. The fresh air was like ambrosia.

"Thanks," I said. And then, wanting to get away from

the Collective Unconscious, I murmured, "There was something I wanted to ask you today."

Dr. Waingloss' eyes glittered. He raised his pencil stub over his pad. "Yes?"

"Well . . . what I wanted to ask you was this. Do you think it's unhealthy to be a virgin?"

"For whom?" Dr. Waingloss inquired.

"I don't know," I said evasively. "For anyone. What I mean is, do you think a lack of sex in a person's life means that there is anything wrong with them?"

"What kind of sex are we discussing?"

"I don't know what kind of sex. Any kind of sex."

"What comes up about sex?" he asked. "What surfaces?"

"*Nothing* comes up about it. That's why I'm bringing it up."

"Free-associate," said Dr. Waingloss, forgetting all about the Collective Unconscious. "What comes to your mind when I say the words sex, love, devotion, marriage?"

"Elephants," I said.

Dr. Waingloss looked startled. "Elephants?"

"Well, yes. In the sense that they're supposed to be very shy about lovemaking and I always thought that was nice. What I mean is, they have a very great sense of privacy. In the jungle and everything."

Dr. Waingloss sighed and gazed at the picture on his desk that showed an elderly woman with bangs. For a second he seemed to forget all about me as he contemplated this woman who so strongly resembled a sheepdog.

115

I decided to take a leap into the unknown. "Is that your wife?" I asked.

His face went as rigid as concrete. "Why do you ask that?"

"I don't know. Just curious."

Dr. Waingloss glared at me. "I am not required to answer personal questions in this office. That is not part of my job."

"Oh," I said. "I'm sorry."

"Nothing in our arrangement here, in the doctor-patient relationship, requires that I answer personal questions."

"OK," I said. "OK. I understand."

"I'm afraid that you do *not* understand," he said angrily. "We are here to discuss you, not me. I am the doctor and you are the patient."

"Look—I'm sorry I brought the whole thing up. I know that I'm the patient and you are the doctor."

"I'm afraid that you don't know," he said, sounding more and more hysterical. "I'm afraid that I have failed to make myself clear on many issues. This is undoubtedly my fault, but . . ."

"Look," I said, "let's go back to the Collective Unconscious. I'm sorry I upset you."

"*Upset me?* It is you who are upset. And if I may say so, I have been very disappointed in your progress these past two months. Very disappointed."

"I'm sorry."

"A psychiatrist goes through a long training before he

116

is allowed to treat patients," said Dr. Waingloss. "Of all the medical disciplines, psychiatry is perhaps the most rigorous, the most demanding."

I was beginning to feel a bit worried about Dr. Waingloss. He seemed to be flipping out.

"It's OK," I said gently. "Everything is going to be OK. I'm sorry I asked you a personal question and I apologize. I'll talk about sex and marriage if you want to. Really."

His face relaxed a little. He gazed at the floor. "Very well, then. Very well."

I felt like I was dealing with a child. "Do you want me to free-associate about elephants?" I asked.

"If you want to," he said. "If the elephant *symbolizes* something for you."

"Oh, it does," I said. "It does."

And so, with a mental sigh, I went into a long treatise about the elephant as sex-symbol, about elephant husbands and elephant wives. About unfaithful elephants. Gay elephants. Elephants who want to be zebras. And all the time I was talking, half of me was thinking about Harold Murth and my virginity, and what a disadvantage the latter was. Harold was thirty years old and had doubtless sown many wild oats in his youth. I had not even sown a cornflake.

14

Harold Murth was missing. For two whole days he had not shown up for his poetry class at 8:45. For two whole days we had had a substitute teacher.

"Where *is* he?" I said to Marylou. "I'm going crazy."

"Out of town," she said calmly. "Visiting his mother. It could be anything."

Which was, indeed, the trouble. Anything could be keeping Harold away from school—and this anything might just possibly be a female. Had Harold fallen in love and lost all control? Eloped with an older woman? Was he, at this very moment, in the violent throes of an affair? I felt like I was going insane.

My pursuit of Harold Murth had gone very badly in the last week. Having sent him 1) a basket of fruit from Charles & Co. 2) a gift certificate from Scribner's 3) some handsome coffee mugs from Jensen's 4) a box of men's toiletries from Caswell-Massey 5) a recording of Judith Anderson reading the poems of John Donne—after having sent him all these things, I had merely received an icy note in the mail.

Dear Miss McAllister,

I am grateful for the many presents you have showered upon me lately, but in view of the fact that our relationship is an academic one, I must ask you to desist.

Yours,

H. Murth

And now Harold Murth was missing. Gone. Fired, perhaps, from the halls of Miss Howlett's. Or had he quit? Had he and Miss Howlett—who was ninety years old and only visited the school once a week—quarreled? It was all too likely, since Miss Howlett was a difficult woman. (This staunch lady, who deserves a book of her own, was one of the few women who had served in the British Royal Air Force in World War I. Evidently she had never gotten over it, since her clothes were entirely military and her personal manner almost Prussian. Appearing at the school each Friday in a brass-buttoned overcoat and fedora hat, she would make the entire school line up in the gymnasium and, striding past the line of girls, would review us like troops. "Posture, my girl!" she would say to an unfortunate seventh grader, poking her in the stomach. "Neatness!" she would shout at a sloppy freshman whose shoelaces were untied. Trying not to giggle, the school would remain at attention while she inspected every single girl, shouting and barking her commands. Why Miss Howlett had ever founded a school for girls rather than, say, a flying academy, was uncertain. One had only to glance at her to envision her sitting in the cockpit of a single-engine

119

plane, her right hand raised in a jaunty salute. I, having hated her in the beginning, was now quite fascinated by her military coats, her plaid capes and rakish hats, and longed to know her better.)

Finally, in the midst of my despair, I decided to approach Esther Tilley. Miss Tilley and I had not spoken more than three words to each other since the afternoon when I had gotten her drunk at Schrafft's. Hoping that this episode was at last fading from her mind, I approached her in the library. "Miss Tilley?" I said.

She turned from the book she was putting back on the shelf. "Oh. J.F. What is it?"

"How have you been, Miss Tilley?" I asked, trying to soften her up a little.

"Well," said Miss Tilley. "And you?"

"Well," I replied. "Very very well. We haven't seen much of each other lately, have we?"

"No," she said stonily. "We haven't."

I decided to plunge into the center of my topic, rather than beat around the bush. "Miss Tilley, I have been rather concerned about Mr. Murth. He hasn't been in class for two days. Do you know where he is?"

Esther Tilley eyed me coolly. "Mr. Murth, I believe, has the flu."

"*What?*" I said.

"He has the flu," repeated Miss Tilley. "I called him last night and he reported to me that his temperature was very high."

I felt like fainting. Screaming. Calling an ambulance.

120

Harold Murth had been ill for two days and I hadn't even known it. I tried to steady my shaking voice. "Thank you, Miss Tilley. I appreciate the information."

It was only one o'clock in the afternoon and I still had two more classes, but I turned on my heel and left the school. Marylou watched me go, amazed, since you could catch hell for doing such a thing. *Screw* the school, I thought as I jumped into a cab. Harold may be dying.

Following my orders, the cab driver sped towards 94th Street. "It's an emergency," I had told him. "Illness." And when we pulled up in front of Harold's house, I thrust a bill at him and didn't even wait for change. By some accident of fate, the usually-locked front door was not locked at all. I raced up the stairs, taking them two at a time.

Once in front of Harold's door, I paused to catch my breath and rearrange my rumpled school uniform. My hair was standing on end, so I smoothed it down. Then I rang the bell.

After what seemed like hours, I heard someone shuffling towards the door. There was a pause and I heard a weak cough. Slowly, the door opened.

"Mr. Murth?" I said. "It's me. J.F. McAllister."

Harold looked stunned. But more than that, he looked ill. Very very ill. His face was flushed and his eyes were glazed, and he seemed unsteady on his feet. He was wearing a long plaid bathrobe.

"Miss McAllister?" he said weakly.

I forced my way into the room. "What is the meaning

121

of all this? You look terrible. How high is your temperature?"

"Miss McAllister . . ."

"Get back into bed," I said sternly. "This is a terrible situation. You look awful."

With gentle pushes, I propelled Harold back to the bedroom. He seemed totally dazed.

"Have you seen a doctor?" I asked.

"I . . ."

"Where is your thermometer?" I demanded.

"In the kitchen," he whispered, collapsing against the pillows.

I marched into the kitchen and found the thermometer. Then I marched back to the bedroom and shook the thermometer vigorously. "Put this under your tongue," I commanded. "Is there any juice in the refrigerator?"

Weakly, Harold shook his head.

"What about Listerine? Aspirin? Nose drops? Kleenex?"

Sadly, Harold shook his head again.

"This is ridiculous. Here you are with the flu, and not a thing in the house. It's ridiculous!"

I removed the thermometer from Harold's mouth. It read 101.

"You have a very high temperature," I said. "You need soups and juices, aspirin every three hours and Listerine. Now, I am going out to get these things, and I do not want you to *budge* until I return."

Harold looked at me in a daze. "Miss McAllister . . ."

"And my name isn't Miss McAllister. It's J.F. I'll be back in ten minutes."

Leaving Harold's door ajar, I raced down to the street. There was a drugstore on the corner, where I purchased five dollars' worth of medical supplies. At a supermarket next door I bought soups and juices, yogurt, tea. Then I hurried back to the apartment.

Harold's eyes were closed. I noticed that there was a great pile of papers and books on the floor, as though he had been working.

I opened a can of pineapple juice and poured him a large glass. "I am surprised at you," I said. "A grown man unable to take care of himself. Now, drink that juice."

Harold obeyed. After which, I gave him two aspirins. Then I sat down and stared at him.

"How do you feel?" I asked.

"Terrible," he said in a muffled voice.

"Do you want me to call a doctor? I know a lot of doctors."

"No, no," Harold said faintly. "I'm not that ill."

"You are *very* ill. And I might never have known it. I might never have gotten here."

"I don't know what to say," he said helplessly.

"There is nothing to say. It is just completely evident that you don't know how to take care of yourself. That's all."

"But I *do*," he whispered. "I jog. I eat health foods . . ."

"Agreed. But your refrigerator is empty, and this place is as cold as Alaska. Why don't they give you more heat?"

To my utter amazement, a tear rolled down Harold's face and landed in his pineapple juice. "I don't know," he said. "There's never been enough heat."

I wanted to put my arms around him, to hug him until he was asphyxiated. But I didn't. "Don't worry about it," I said harshly. "I'll talk to the landlord. It'll be OK."

"You are very kind," he whispered.

A mass of turbulent feelings swept through me like a storm. "Sleep," I said gruffly. "Rest. I'll sit in the living room."

So for the next two hours I sat on the one chair in the living room while Harold dozed. I was close to tears, yet furious at the same time. Harold Murth was about as capable of taking care of himself as Marylou's brother Nelson. As a matter of fact, he reminded me of Nelson very much. Only Nelson would weep into a glass of pineapple juice. Only Nelson would wear a bathrobe that was two sizes too large. But who would have thought that Harold Murth would be so frail? Did I like him this way, I asked myself. Yes, I told myself, I did.

Around 4:30 I tiptoed back into the bedroom. Harold's eyes were open and he attempted a smile. "Hello."

"Hi," I said. "I'm going to cook you some soup."

He gazed at me with the grateful eyes of a basset hound. "I don't know what to say. You've been so thoughtful."

"You need someone to look after you," I muttered, staring at the floor.

Harold looked as innocent as a child. "I do?"

"Yeah, you do." And then there was a silence. "I guess

you're wondering why I came here today."

"I *did* wonder," Harold said faintly. "It was such a surprise."

I decided to take a mad plunge. And if I drowned, I drowned. "Well," I said, "the reason I'm here is the same reason I sent you those presents. I mean, that's the reason. And maybe when your temperature goes down you'll be able to figure it out. Now, I want you to take some more aspirin and then I'll cook the soup. I got a very good kind called Campbell's Chunky Chicken."

Harold's limpid eyes glanced briefly into mine, and then fluttered away. "You are very kind," he said. "Very very kind."

15

"It is important to remember," said Harold Murth, "that James Oppenheim thought of himself as a prophet, a Whitmanesque champion of the downtrodden. It was doubtless his settlement work and teaching on the Lower East Side that gave his poems such a strong sociological cast. This, combined with his Jewish ancestry, makes his voice a distinct one in the period we are discussing."

I stared at Harold Murth as he spoke over our heads into the air. Was it possible that only two weeks ago I had been nursing him through a grave illness? Was it possible that for three entire afternoons I had cooked his meals, made him take aspirin and gargle with Listerine? Was it possible that all these things had transpired only for the two of us to wind up strangers? It was fantastic. The moment he had come back to school the old barriers had returned. Meeting me in the corridor, he had nodded and hurried onward. Noticing my intense gaze in class, he had averted his eyes. Once again I was "Miss McAllister." Once again we were teacher and pupil, adolescent and adult.

I cast my mind back over the three glorious days I had spent with him. Three days of plumping up pillows, cooking soup and taking his temperature. Three days of forging my mother's handwriting on her engraved stationery and sending messages to the school with the news that J.F. McAllister was having dental work done and could not attend classes. Three days of being close to Harold and studying his possessions—an ascetic collection of dime-store crockery, first editions, and bath towels that unexpectedly said "Holiday House Motel." There was not a single aspect of his life that did not mesmerize me. The military cleanliness of his home. The bare refrigerator. The portrait of Christopher Smart gazing insanely onto 94th Street.

My heart had pounded as I marched in and out of Harold's bedroom, words of love thudding through my mind like clumsy acrobats. My face had flushed whenever he said "Thank you, J.F." or "You are very kind." It was amazing how different he was from the Harold Murth I had imagined, how vulnerable and Nelson-like. And yet, in spite of these revelations about his character I loved him more than ever. The way his illness rendered him utterly helpless. The way he wrinkled up his nose when he drank unsweetened grapefruit juice.

Since Harold's illness had caused him to fall asleep constantly, we had talked but little. Yet what was there to say? He had needed me and I had responded to the need. It reminded me of scenes from World War II movies. A wounded Van Johnson being nursed by a tough, yet secretly tender Rosalind Russell.

And now it was over. Concluded. The end.

127

I tore a piece of paper out of my notebook and wrote a message to Marylou, who was sitting nearby.

What the hell is going on? *He acts*
like he's never seen me before.

Marylou wrote on the bottom of the page.

I've told you a hundred times. He's very shy.

Fine. Wonderful. But words like these did not assuage my grief over the fact that Harold Murth and I were strangers again. What was there to be done? Kidnap him in the faculty cloakroom? Attack him in the vestibule of his apartment house? No. There was nothing to be done.

Marylou wrote me another note and passed it over.

Can you baby-sit with Nelson tonight?
My parents are going out, and I have a lecture
at the Museum of Natural History.

I nodded at Marylou, despite the fact that Nelson—in large doses—got on my nerves. What the hell. I might as well sit and watch television with him as sit and watch it at home. Life, I thought. Life. Life stank.

(A pause here for Marylou and her lectures. They drove me crazy, yet they were such an integral part of her life that I never had the heart to criticize them. She attended lectures all over the city—dissertations on Egypt and the pyramids, slide-shows on Stonehenge, travel films on the Orient. She went to lectures on pre-Columbian art at the Metropolitan and lectures on medieval music at the Cloisters. And to this day I can see her flying off to one of these events wearing a shabby camel's-hair coat—a red scarf around her neck and her brown bangs plastered limply against her forehead. I see her rushing to catch the Fifth Avenue bus and then turning back to wave at me. I see her crooked smile and love her all over again.)

Later that evening Nelson and I sat in the Browns' living room watching a game show on TV. Some addled blonde had just won a motorboat by identifying a piece of music by Cole Porter, but I did not care. Nor did I care that Nelson was in one of his unbearably sweet moods, holding my hand on the sofa and offering me sips of his Coke. We had both eaten so many pretzels from a cellophane bag that I felt ill.

How are you going to raise that thousand bucks by Christmas? I asked myself. Today is the 16th of December and you are not even up to eight hundred. Nor have you done your Christmas shopping. Nor have you done any homework since October. What is the matter with you? Why aren't you more organized? Everyone else gets things done and goes to bed at reasonable hours. But *you* are running around like a chicken with its head off and you are not going to rake in that thousand bucks by Christmas. You have failed.

I glared at Nelson, suddenly furious that he was keeping me from working the theatre district. It was Thursday night, and I always did well on Thursdays. It was fortunate that the nights were picking up because the days, on Fifth Avenue, had begun to be lousy. There was just too much competition. The Salvation Army singing their endless Christmas carols. Santas recruited from the Bowery, smelling of whiskey and saying "Ho, ho, ho." God—there were even *girl* Santas this year, collecting for various charities and looking absolutely adorable in their little Santa costumes, minus beards. The Christmas confusion among the street peddlers and musicians was extreme, there being too many of us in the first place, and I had begun to notice that all those without licenses had a friend posted as lookout. George, for example—who sold the leather belts—had a girl working with him who stood on top of the trash receptacle on the corner of 49th and scanned the avenue for cops. "Cheeze it!" she would yell when she spotted one of the men in blue. "The fuzz!" And George—and others like him—would quickly bundle up their wares and depart. I, on the other hand, had only to slip my harmonica into my pocket and merge with the crowd. It was a rough way to make a living, I had decided, unless you were established and licensed like Benny Goldstein.

Damn you, I thought, gazing at Nelson. Without you I could be working Shubert Alley tonight. Without you I could take in a fast twenty bucks.

And then the idea hit me.

"Nelson . . ." I said.

"Yes?" he said, his mouth full of pretzels. "Yes, J.F.?"

"How would you like to go out tonight?"

130

He turned his angelic face towards me, all twinkles and surprise. "Out?"

"Yes," I said. "Out. For an outing. Outdoors."

"That would be nice," he said. "Is it going to snow?"

I tried to control my rage. "I don't know, Nelson, but I certainly hope not. Because I want you to help me with something."

Nelson's face suddenly became serious. Determined. "I'll help you," he said.

"You don't even know what it is yet."

"It doesn't matter," he said, taking my hand. "I'll help."

"OK then. Here's the problem. I've bet one of the kids at school that I can make twenty bucks playing the harmonica on the street at night. You know. Like a street musician or something. So I'd like you to come with me and pass the hat. It'll be our secret. OK?"

"Gee," he said, "that's a neat idea, J.F. What will we do with the money?"

For a moment he had me stumped. "Well . . . we'll buy candy and pretzels with some of it. And then I'll keep the rest."

"Neat," said Nelson. "That's a neat idea."

"There's just one thing," I said.

"Yes?"

"I want you to wear your oldest clothes. Because if we look rich or something, people won't give us money."

"Right," he said, sounding like an accomplice in a murder. "Right. I gotcha."

Thirty minutes later Nelson and I were in a cab, heading for Shubert Alley. I was quite pleased with the way he looked—tiny faded blue jeans and a worn duffle coat. It was beginning to snow, but what the hell. I had played in inclement weather before. Too much snow, however, and the harmonica tended to go slightly flat.

Nelson and I set up shop in front of the Booth Theatre. An English mystery was playing but the sidewalk was deserted because it wasn't yet time for intermission. "I will start playing when the people come out for intermission," I instructed Nelson. "I want you to look very sad and pathetic and go around passing the hat. Right?"

"Right," said Nelson. "Gotcha."

I warmed up with a few scales and pretty soon the doors opened and people started drifting out onto the street, lighting cigarets. They were a rich-looking crowd and many of them, I noticed with pleasure, were high. People always gave me more money when they were plastered.

I whipped into my medley of English Folk Songs—to go with the English play inside—and was pleased to see several one-dollar bills flutter into the hat. Nelson, a born actor, seemed to grow even smaller than he was. He wandered among the crowd passing the hat and smiling shyly. "My little brother," I told a lady who was standing nearby. She gave me a look of compassion and put two bucks into Nelson's hat. Then Nelson started to improvise. "Please help my sister," he said in a tiny voice. "My sister is very poor."

I felt like kicking him in the behind. But miraculously, his words had the desired effect. Dollar bills were now

132

fluttering into the hat as though there were no tomorrow, and for a moment I envisioned a terrific future for Nelson and me. The Dynamic Duo. We really did look perfect. Pathetic yet brave. Poor but intelligent.

"Please help my sister," wailed Nelson. "It's snowing and my sister is very poor."

And then a number of things went wrong. Very wrong.

The first thing that went wrong was that my parents came out of the theatre. And the second thing that went wrong was that Nelson's parents came out of the theatre. And then everything went wrong because out of the theatre came 1) Miss Howlett 2) Esther Tilley 3) five other teachers from my school. How could I have forgotten? It was December 16th. And the performance of the English mystery was, that night, being given as a benefit for Miss Howlett's adoption agency.

The first people to notice me were my parents. And the second people to notice me were Nelson's parents. And then, it seemed, everyone noticed me and started talking all at once. Their voices rose into the air in a cacophonous flurry, mingling with snow and cigaret smoke. Passersby began to stare.

It went on and on. Samuel and Bradley Brown grabbed Nelson and shoved him into a cab, shouting at me that it was snowing and that he would probably catch pneumonia. And then my mother grabbed me by the neck and shook me as though I were a Raggedy Andy doll. Miss Howlett, who was the only one to keep her cool, kept saying, "Is that one of *my* girls? How extraordinary."

133

I went home in a cab with my parents—and refused to say a word. I refused to say why I was playing the harmonica on the street for money, why Nelson was with me, or indeed, what the entire thing meant. I was mum, silent, mute. I would not utter a syllable.

"Suppose I had been with business colleagues!" shouted my father.

"Suppose my friends had seen you!" screamed my mother.

"Don't you realize that you are a girl from a good family?" my father yelled.

"An *important* family," my mother echoed.

"What is the matter with you?" said my father. "Isn't your allowance large enough? Don't we give you everything?"

"A girl who has gone to the best schools . . ." moaned my mother.

"The best summer camps . . ." echoed my father.

"My lips are sealed," I declared.

And they were. Despite their threats and entreaties. Despite the fact that they were so personally wounded by what I had done that they could hardly contain themselves. *Their* daughter had been caught begging on the street. *Their* child had disgraced them.

Man, I thought, as I lay in bed that night, I am never going to become a parent. Wow. What an ego-trip. What a false sense of possession. Man. And now working the street is out. O.U.T. A beautiful career gone down the drain. A terrific talent smashed. Damn it to hell. *How* am I going to raise that thousand bucks?

16

It was Saturday and I was under house arrest. All my harmonicas had been taken away, my allowance had been docked again, and I was in complete disgrace. My mother, who had been out late the night before, was still asleep. My father was at his club. In the deep recesses of the apartment I could hear Bertha, our housekeeper, running the vacuum cleaner.

I stood by the window of my room, chain-smoking and watching snow cascade into the courtyard. A small sooty bird sat on the windowsill eyeing the weather. Far down Park Avenue there was the distant wail of a fire engine.

For the third time that morning, I decided to phone Marylou.

"Hi," I said. "It's me again."

"I know," she said wearily. "Can't you find anything to do?"

"No. All I can think about are my harmonicas. God. It's like taking a person's *underwear* away or something. I mean, it's so personal."

"She'll give them back."

"Who knows? Maybe she won't. Maybe she'll hock them."

"You're being facetious."

"You're right—that's what I'm being. Listen, how is Nelson's cold?"

"Not too bad. My mother's keeping him in bed."

"I guess she'll never forgive me."

Marylou sighed. "She'll forgive you, J.F. Everyone will forgive you in time."

"I feel bad about the whole thing."

"I know."

There was a pause on the phone, but not an uncomfortable one.

"It was weird about Miss Howlett, wasn't it?" I said.

"Not really," said Marylou. "She's very eccentric."

"I wish you could have been there. It was like a scene from a play."

The episode I was referring to had occurred the morning after my harmonica-disaster. Dashing into school that A.M. I had been told that Miss Howlett wanted to see me in her office. My heart had frozen as I took the tiny elevator up to the fifth floor because I was sure that I was about to be expelled. Despite its liberated curriculum, Miss Howlett's school was still very old-fashioned. Girls from Miss Howlett's did *not* play harmonicas on the street.

I knocked on the door and after a pregnant pause Miss Howlett's English voice shouted, "Enter!"

"Good morning, Miss Howlett," I said.

She was sitting at her desk wearing a black cape, a monocle and a riding hat. She did not look ninety years old. She looked terrific. "Jacqueline McAllister?" she inquired loudly.

136

I trembled slightly. "Yes, ma'am. That's me."

"Come in," she said.

"Thank you," I said.

"You are in the eleventh grade?" she demanded. "One of our juniors?"

"Yes, ma'am."

Miss Howlett glanced at a file card on her desk. "And you have been attending this school since the seventh grade?"

"Yes, ma'am."

"Extraordinary," she said.

"Yes," I said.

She stared at me through her monocle. "You are, I believe, the young person who was playing the mouth organ last night. On the street."

My heart sank. "Yes, ma'am."

"And collecting money at the same time? In a hat?"

"Yes."

Miss Howlett contemplated me—as though I had two heads. "You were collecting for charity?"

"No, ma'am."

"For some worthy cause?"

"No, ma'am. For myself."

"And you consider this proper behavior for a Howlett girl?"

I stared at the floor. "No, ma'am."

"Do you know what year this school was founded?" she inquired.

My heart sank lower. "No, ma'am. I don't."

"It was founded in 1922, and its motto was then—as it

137

is now—'Seek, and ye shall find.' The words, of course, referred to education, to knowledge, to self-improvement."

"Yes, ma'am."

"Knowledge was the first aim of this institution," she declared. "The second was deportment—the instrument through which adolescent savages were to be transformed into human beings."

"Yes, ma'am," I said. My voice had sunk to a whisper.

"Now," said Miss Howlett, "I fail to see how begging on the street, in the theatre district of this city, could improve either your knowledge or your deportment. I fail to see how it could assist you in becoming a human being, and I very *seriously* fail to see how it could reflect the aims of this school."

"It wasn't for myself," I whispered.

"What!" she bellowed. "Speak up, girl! Can't hear you."

"It wasn't for myself," I said desperately. "I was doing it for . . . a friend."

Miss Howlett removed her monocle. "You will explain yourself."

"I can't," I said miserably. "I'm sorry. It's private."

All of a sudden a light came into Miss Howlett's eye. "Would I be right in conjecturing that you were doing it for a young man?"

I was stunned. "Well . . . yes. In a way."

She leaned forward. "And would I be right in conjecturing that this young man is at the moment financially embarrassed?"

138

I was amazed. "Well . . . yes."

Miss Howlett sighed and stared out of the window. Her ferocity seemed to melt away—like the air going out of a tire. "I was in the British Royal Air Force. Did you know that?"

"Yes," I said in a small voice. "I've heard about it."

"The only woman to fly in the First War," she mused. "My God, what times we had. Every mission might be your last so you lived life to the hilt. Tasted the very last drop of it. Incredible experience."

My mind hurried back to old movies with Frederic March in them. Camaraderie in the trenches. Shell-shock. Jerries and doughboys. I pictured Miss Howlett in uniform.

Her thoughts were far away now, lingering over the past. "*My* young man was a flier—and a damned good one—but on one particular mission . . . well, he lost his nerve. Went to pieces. Could happen to anyone, of course. The very best of 'em faltered at times. . . . So I took his plane and went up for him—into a swarm of Jerries. Against all the rules, you understand. Could have been cashiered for such a thing. But I thought to myself, 'Blast the rules. Neville needs me.' So I flew his mission, and survived, and no one ever knew the difference. . . . Poor old Neville. He had had much too soft a life. The father titled and all that. And the mother grew roses. Never knew such a silly woman. Spent her whole life growing roses and playing with the dogs. Damned house smelled like a kennel. . . . Now *my* people were a different sort.

139

Military chaps, all of 'em. No time for gardening and croquet. Too busy defending the Empire. . . ." Her voice softened. "He married someone else, of course. Neville, I mean." Miss Howlett shook herself awake. "What were we talking about?"

"Me," I said in a small voice.

"Ah yes," she declared. "You and your young man. Love him, do you?"

"Yes," I mumbled, staring at the floor.

"Then don't let 'em stop you!" she said fiercely. "Stick to your guns! Do your own . . ." She hesitated.

"Thing?" I suggested.

"Right," she concurred. "Do your own thing. Amazing expression, but accurate. Off with you now. I don't have all day."

To my surprise, I saluted her. "Yes, ma'am!"

"One moment," she barked, as I turned to the door.

I froze in my tracks. "Yes?"

She gave me the very slightest of smiles, and then it disappeared. "You're damned good on that mouth organ, you know. Keep practicing."

I grinned at her. "Thank you, Miss Howlett. I will."

At any rate, I spent that Saturday mooching about the house, and phoning Marylou, and inquiring after Nelson's health. I went to bed early and woke up, amazingly, at 5 A.M. on Sunday. It was the earliest I'd been up for a long time so I decided to clean out my closet and listen to the radio. I padded silently into the kitchen for a mug of coffee, padded back, and then removed every single item from the closet. It was a weird assortment. Ten pairs of faded Levi's, four Windbreakers, a fishing rod, a lot of winter coats and a hockey stick. I dove deeper into the closet and found a stamp album that had been missing for years and a single snowshoe. Where had I gotten *that*, I wondered.

The radio was playing Christmas carols, which depressed the hell out of me, but then it switched to a religious program. "This is 'The Voice of Faith,' " said the announcer. "And the word for Christmas is Murth."

I dropped the snowshoe I had been holding and listened in amazement.

"How many of us," asked the announcer, "know the real secret of Murth? The secret of joy? How many of us know that to experience Murth is to become a little child again, as our Savior was a child. The word for Christmas, dear friends, is Murth. Murth and Murth alone is the secret of the holiday season."

I might have had a religious conversion on the spot except for the fact that it dawned on me that he was saying "mirth" instead of "Murth." Ah well, I thought, the English language is strange.

The next day was Monday—the last day of school before Christmas vacation—and I woke up so depressed that I considered doing away with myself. Two weeks of Christmas holidays. Two weeks of not seeing Harold. His behavior towards me had grown so cold, so utterly aloof, that I was beginning to think that he had resented my nursing him through the flu. Perhaps I had seen the whole thing through rose-colored glasses. Perhaps my presence during those days had merely been an intrusion on his life.

As usual I was going to be late for school, so I raced into my clothes, sped down in the elevator, briefly greeted Jim Ryan our doorman, and hailed a cab. It had finally occurred to me that for what I spent on cabs a person could emigrate to New Zealand. But I could not help it. I was always late.

Harold's class was just starting as I raced into the classroom and slid into my seat. Marylou, already in place, gazed at me and shook her head. Her expression meant, "I love you, J.F., but you need a keeper."

I stared at Harold, amazed at how beautiful he looked. He was wearing his sand-colored tweed jacket and gray trousers. His hair looked soft and fluffy, as though he had just washed it, and his smooth skin was shining pink. I fixed him with a steady gaze. I love you, the gaze said, and I am going to love you for the rest of my life. I am not going to fall out of love, or change my mind, or love someone else when I get older. I love *you*—you, Harold Murth, and if you were smart you would take advantage of it. I am a terrific person to have around the house, not just when a person is sick but at other times. I am very mechanical. I can fix washers on faucets and pilot lights on stoves and electrical sockets. When I was nine years old they gave me an aptitude test in school and the results were that, while I was incredibly poor at words, numbers, logic and spelling, I did have the mechanical abilities of a man of forty. I love you, Harold Murth. Why can't you love me back?

Harold gazed into the air, far above our heads, and quoted a poem by David Morton—another poet I had never heard of.

Mortality upon these slender forms
Is all too heavy with its weight of change,
Too desperately sweet with little storms
Troubling the flesh within its little range.

I listened to Harold recite, my mind lapsing into an unreal state—half waking, half dream. I saw Harold and me walking by a Scottish lake, huge swans gliding past us. I saw us sitting in a dimly-lit French café, gazing into each other's eyes. I saw us in sunny Greece, standing in the Parthenon. In my dazed mind we travelled to Moscow, Naples and Ceylon.

And then the class was over and I woke up.

Harold cleared his throat nervously. "This is our last session before the Christmas holidays," he said, "and so I would like to wish you all the very best tidings of the season. Let us meet again in January with renewed vigor, renewed dedication. I have enjoyed the semester very much."

There was a vague mumble of appreciation from the girls, and then they fled. To the washroom. To the library. To other classes. Later that day we were having a Christmas program in the auditorium, presided over by Miss Howlett, and everyone was looking forward to it because a couple of celebrities who had once attended the school were going to speak.

I stared at Harold Murth for one last time, and then I left the room. I did not wish him a Merry Christmas or even a Happy New Year. I was too depressed.

I went to my other classes, had a miserable lunch, and gave Marylou a pre-Christmas present I had bought for her—a book on mummies. She gave me a plastic carrying bag for the back of my bike. These early presents were a kind of tradition between us.

Then it was time for the Christmas program. Disconsolately, I moved down the crowded hallway towards the auditorium, fighting my way through the mass of girls. Exuberant seventh and eighth graders shrieked with the joy of the holiday season. Older girls giggled and gossiped. I noticed, with a little pang, that Harold was walking right in front of me.

We were just passing the biology lab when Harold reached in his pocket, crumpled up an envelope and threw it into the trash receptacle. Amazed at myself, I stopped in my tracks, made sure he was out of sight, and then retrieved the envelope. It had belonged to him. I wanted it.

The front of the envelope was addressed to him and bore the words "New York Telephone Company" in the upper left-hand corner. Then I turned it over and received a shock. On the back of the envelope someone had written, over and over, the words "J.F. McAllister." My name, in fact, had been turned into an elaborate doodle interlaced with birds, flowers, and trees.

And it was Harold Murth who had written it.

17

Harold Murth loved me. I was so sure of it that I had framed the New York Telephone Company envelope and hung it over my bed. Harold loved me, me J.F. McAllister, a person no man had ever loved before. Why else would he doodle my name all over an envelope? The only name *I* had ever doodled all over an envelope was Greta Garbo's, during the year that I was enamored of her. My passion for doodling her name, as a matter of fact, had evolved into a kind of graffiti with the words "Greta Garbo" sprouting unexpectedly in buses and in ladies' rooms and on the side of buildings. And this, mind you, years before graffiti became the thing.

Harold Murth loved me. But, my God, when had it all begun? With his having the flu? Perhaps he had fallen in love with me at the beginning of the semester and avoided me out of sheer fright. Harold Murth was very shy, very reticent. If he loved someone, he would never let her know it. But I would let *him* know everything. I would go to his house on Christmas Eve with a bottle of champagne and reveal myself. But I needed that thousand bucks.

I locked my bedroom door and dialed Marylou's number.

"I'm desperate," I explained. "Now that I know he loves me I feel that everything should be brought out into the open. And then we can elope or something."

"Yes?" said Marylou, waiting for the axe to fall.

"But I need that thousand bucks. And I've only got eight hundred."

Marylou sighed. "It would wipe me out, J.F. And Nelson too. Between us, two hundred is exactly the amount we have in the bank."

"I'll pay you back," I said fervently. "I swear on my honor, I'll pay you back."

"I'd have to do it without telling him. Nelson, I mean. He'd be so upset."

"I'll pay him interest. But I have got to show up at Harold's on Christmas Eve with a bottle of champagne and the check. I've planned it that way."

"All right," she said, "I'll do it. But no one must ever know."

"I swear," I said passionately.

There was a pause, and then Marylou said gently, "J.F., maybe we should do something about your looks."

"My looks?" I said. "What's the matter with my looks? My *looks*? I look fine."

"Of course you do," she said kindly. "To us. But to the rest of the world . . ."

I felt a pang inside me. "I never thought you would say such a thing Marylou. It's incredible. I mean it."

"But if you're going to spend an evening with Harold . . ."

"Spend an *evening* with him," I said angrily. "I'm going to seduce him."

There was a shocked silence. And then Marylou, rising above everything she believed in, said, "Well, if that is the case, then you'd better look like a girl."

So the following day we took my mother's charge plate and went to Lord & Taylor. It was incredible how women dressed, I thought to myself, as Marylou guided me around the store. So impractically. Everything for show and nothing you could even play baseball in. Long flowered dresses. Bell-bottom pants. Shoes with Wedgie-type heels. Wow, what a circus. Nevertheless. Marylou is probably right in feeling that on this one occasion you should look like a female. It will ease the way.

(My decision to seduce Harold on Christmas Eve had not been made lightly. Only sex, I had decided, could break the ice that shone so coldly between us. Only sex could make us forget that we were teacher and pupil, adolescent and adult. Only sex could render our relationship chatty and comfortable. In my mind's eye I saw us lying in bed smoking cigarets and talking about our lives, sharing confidences. The only trouble was that my mind's eye could not get our clothes off. We lay in bed completely dressed.)

I was not exactly sure how you seduced someone, but felt—from watching old movies with Nelson—that it had to do with lighting, ambiance, two sparkling glasses of champagne and a single rose in a vase. I saw Paul Henreid smiling across a candlelit table at Bette Davis. I saw Ingrid

Bergman drinking cocktails with Cary Grant. There should be music on the radio, soft carpeting, and snow falling gently outside. Could any of these things be accomplished in Harold's bare apartment? God. Perhaps he didn't even *own* a radio.

I am about to lose my virginity, I thought. I am about to dispense with the whole damn thing. Good. It's time. In February I will be seventeen. And who ever heard of a seventeen-year-old virgin in the city of New York?

After hours of shopping, Marylou and I finally chose a pair of black velvet bell-bottom pants, a white silk blouse and a pair of patent leather shoes. I didn't look too bad in this outfit, if I did say so myself. It wasn't really *me,* but on the other hand, the person it was was rather interesting. A stylish young woman of Manhattan. A sort of lady executive type.

Marylou and I trooped homeward on the Madison Avenue bus. She had promised to wash and set my hair the following day, so all in all I felt pretty good. By tomorrow evening I would be in Harold Murth's arms.

My coiffure wasn't as easy as Marylou thought—my hair being so short—but after much washing and drying and teasing, we did come up with something that made up in height what it lacked in style. I donned my new outfit and gazed at myself in the mirror. My parents were at a Christmas Eve party, so Marylou and I had the apartment to ourselves.

"I am lacking one thing," I said to her. "Only one thing."

148

Marylou was sitting on my bed, studying me. "What's that?" she said.

"A fur coat," I replied. "My mother's wearing her mink tonight, but I could borrow her fake fur. What do you think?"

"You mean the black one with the silver buttons?"

"Right."

"Won't she mind?"

I faced Marylou. "She'll mind, all right. But what the hell."

Feeling like criminals, Marylou and I stole into my mother's bedroom and lifted the coat out of the closet. It looked terrific on me. I looked like the lady president of a corporation.

Marylou circled me slowly, appreciatively. "How do you feel?"

"Well, it's hard to describe," I said. "I mean, it's not me, but it could have been if I had been somebody else. If you see what I mean. *Do* you see what I mean?"

Marylou nodded. She saw.

The last thing we did was adorn me with a tiny bit of eye shadow and mascara, and a dab of Chanel No. 5—and then Marylou escorted me downstairs. Our doorman, Jim Ryan, didn't even recognize me. "A cab, ladies?" he asked, opening the door for us. Feeling a little weird, I nodded and he blew his silver whistle.

And then I was alone—huddled in the back seat of the cab—speeding towards Harold's apartment, a bottle of champagne on the seat beside me and a bank check for a thousand dollars in the pocket of my mother's coat. What are you doing? I asked myself. Suppose you fail?

If you fail, you fail, I muttered. Nothing ventured, nothing gained.

Within a few moments the cab pulled up in front of Harold's house, and, sending a little prayer into the winter sky, I disembarked and tried the front door of the building. Locked. Only momentarily nonplussed, I pushed a buzzer that said "Schwartz" and the Schwartzes, whoever they were, obligingly released the door catch from upstairs. Clutching the bottle of champagne, I made my ascent.

Now, I said to myself as I stood in front of Harold's door, whatever happens you are not going to lose your cool. You are going to behave like an adult and let the chips fall where they may.

I patted my new hairdo into place and knocked loudly. After what seemed an eternity, Harold opened the door and jumped backward a little. He was wearing his bathrobe and slippers.

It was not that he did not recognize me. It was simply that he seemed confused. Very confused. "J.F.?" he said. "Jacqueline? Miss McAllister?"

"Merry Christmas!" I said. "I just happened to be passing and I thought I'd drop in. Happy New Year!"

Before Harold could demur, I hurried into the apartment and surveyed the room. There was a sprig of holly in a vase and a single candle burning. His Christmas decorations.

150

Harold stared at me, looking paler than usual. "Miss McAllister . . . is it you?"

"Well, it was this morning," I said gaily. "So I guess it must be now. *C'est la vie!*"

"You look . . ." Harold averted his eyes nervously. "Different."

"Oh," I said casually, "you mean my clothes. Well, I've been making the rounds of a few parties and you know how the holidays are. You have to dress. A terrible bore, really."

Harold gazed over my head. "Indeed."

"Champagne!" I said cheerfully, waving the bottle in front of him. "A little vino for the holiday season."

"I beg your pardon?" said Harold.

"I brought you a bottle of champagne."

"Champagne?"

"Sure. Piper-Heidsieck. Why not?"

"I don't drink alcohol," Harold stated quietly. "It creates low blood sugar."

"Oh," I said. And then there was one of those terrible pauses.

I decided to shift into another gear. "Well, Mr. Murth, aren't you going to take my coat? I'm kind of warm with it on."

The gambit worked, for Harold was, if nothing else, a gentleman. "Of course," he said. "Do forgive me."

I sat down on the one chair in the living room and lit a cigaret as he hung my coat up. I felt wildly confused, because my clothes were not changing me the way I had

151

hoped. I had been almost positive that the new clothes would create a new me, but I felt exactly the same—like a teen-age cab driver. Losing confidence by the second, I tried to lean nonchalantly back in the chair with my cigaret held at a rakish angle. I crossed my legs and smiled a world-weary smile.

Harold came back into the room and drew his bathrobe around him. He seemed terribly uncomfortable. "I was just about to step into the tub," he stated. "When you knocked, that is."

Great, I felt like saying. Let's step into it together.

"So you must forgive my appearance," Harold concluded.

"Oh, I do," I said. "I mean, it's OK. Really."

Harold cleared his throat and gazed into the air. "I was quite startled by your Christmas present. It arrived yesterday."

(I have not yet mentioned that my choice for Harold's Christmas was not—as I had previously planned—a deluge of gifts, but rather one gift. One exquisite gift from Tiffany's. In other words, I had invaded my savings account, marched into the most intimidating store in New York and bought him a crystal paperweight. Sixty dollars, gift wrapped.)

I looked around the room. "Where is it? The paperweight."

Harold gazed at the ceiling. "It is still in the box, Miss McAllister. I cannot possibly accept such an expensive gift."

Then how are you going to accept one thousand dollars? I asked silently. And how are we going to make love if you continue to stand there hugging your bathrobe? *I love you,* Harold Murth. I would die for you. And there you stand, hugging your bathrobe.

I decided to start over again. From the top. "Look, Mr. Murth, why don't you bring in the stool from the bedroom? I don't like to be the only one sitting down."

"Very well," he replied. "If it would make you more comfortable."

"It would," I said firmly.

Harold got the stool and placed it opposite me. Then he sat down with his knees together—careful to keep the bathrobe wrapped around him.

"Cigaret?" I asked, offering him one.

"I only smoke a pipe," he said.

"Oh. Of course. I forgot."

A number of strategies raced through my mind. The first was to attack him, tearing the bathrobe from his frail body and making love to him. But I knew I wasn't brave enough to do that. The second was to drink the bottle of champagne all by myself—and thus released from inhibition, loosen my clothes and my morals at the same time. But I knew I couldn't do that either. The third strategy was simply to present him with the check and a simple declaration of love, and let him take it from there. He was obviously having a difficult time revealing his love for me, and I had to help him out.

I glanced at the portrait of Christopher Smart, and a

tiny bell rang in my head. "That's a terrific portrait," I said. "I admired it the last time I was here."

Harold looked surprised. "You did?"

"Yeah, I did. What a great poet that guy was."

For the first time since I had arrived, Harold looked awake. "You are familiar with Smart?"

"Familiar?" I said. "He's practically my favorite poet in the world. I think it's awful that he went crazy. Do you think he would have been better off staying at Cambridge? What I mean is, do you think a quiet sort of academic life would have prevented him from losing his mind? Because there is certainly no doubt that he lost it."

Harold looked impressed. "You seem very familiar with him."

I sent up a little prayer of thanks that I had done my homework on Christopher Smart. "Not really. It's just that he's always held a kind of fascination for me. I mean, a guy with such tremendous talent squandering it that way. And then being locked up in an insane asylum and everything. It's tragic."

Harold was staring at me intently. "My thesis is on Smart, you know."

"I know," I said. "I mean, Esther Tilley once mentioned it to me in passing. He's a terrific subject for a thesis."

Harold sighed. "He has been my *raison d'être* for the past ten years, Miss McAllister."

"Madness and Redemption in the Poems of Christopher Smart," I quoted. "It's a neat title."

Harold's eyes widened. "You know the title of my thesis?"

"Well, yes. In a way. I mean, Miss Tilley once mentioned it to me in passing."

Harold was now fully alert, and I knew we were making progress. "Which of his poems impresses you the most, Miss McAllister?"

"Well," I said, "when you come right down to it, it's got to be the *Jubilate Agno.*"

"Correct," said Harold. "I agree."

"Because, though a little crazy, that poem is really original."

"Correct," Harold said.

"Did it really take him four years to write it?"

"It did indeed. But you must remember that he was confined in a madhouse at the time."

" 'For the sun is an intelligence and an angel of the human form,' " I quoted. " 'For the moon is an intelligence and an angel in shape like a woman.' "

Harold looked stunned. "You know the poems by heart?"

"Sure," I said. "Why not? I mean, once you've licked the eighteenth-century idiom you can't help but memorize them. They're so catchy."

Harold drew closer to me. My heart began to pound wildly. "Very few people feel so strongly about Smart," he said. "Actually, you are only the second person I've met who has memorized him. It's extraordinary."

"Who was the first?" I asked.

"My wife," he replied.

For a moment I had no reaction. There was simply a silence in the room, a vast roaring silence which filled my head like an avalanche. And then I said, "Your what?"

"My wife," Harold said calmly. "Margery. She lives in New Jersey."

18

"Miss McAllister!" said Harold. "Are you all right? Can I get you a glass of water?"

"I'm fine," I mumbled, holding onto the sides of the chair.

"But you look ill," Harold protested.

"No, no," I said. "I'm OK. But maybe you'd better open that champagne."

Harold hurried into the kitchen, and after a long pause there was a POP, and he rushed back into the room with a water glass and the bottle of champagne, which was overflowing like a fountain.

"So clumsy of me," he said. "I'm sorry."

"It's OK," I said, pouring myself a tumbler of champagne. "Everything is going to be OK."

I drank the champagne in one gulp and belched. Then I poured myself a second glass. "You want some?" I asked.

Harold shook his head. He looked nervous. "Are you sure you're all right?"

"Terrific," I said. "Wonderful. Never better. What did you say her name was?"

"Margery. Margery Murth."

"Terrific," I said, pouring myself some more champagne. "And where did you say she lived?"

Harold averted his head. "In Tenafly."

"New Jersey?"

"That is correct."

Once again, I belched. "Excuse me for belching," I said.

"That is perfectly all right," Harold replied. And then a silence descended on us. Hold on to yourself, I told myself. This isn't as bad as it seems. You've always known that life stank, so why be surprised.

"I guess you visit her on weekends," I said, trying to sound calm.

"Ah . . . not exactly."

"Holidays, then?"

"No," said Harold. And then there was a pause. "Actually . . ." he declared, "we are separated."

"Separated," I repeated.

"Yes."

My heart rose like a balloon. "Gee. That's a shame."

Harold gazed at the ceiling. "It *has* been a difficult experience."

"Breaking up is rough," I concurred happily.

"Oh, we're not breaking up," said Harold. "At the moment we are in the process of having, ah . . . a little counseling."

"Oh."

"Marriage counseling," Harold explained.

"Oh," I said.

Suddenly he stared me in the face. "We are terribly in

158

love, Miss McAllister. When we separated last August and I came to this apartment, I brought only the barest necessities because the whole thing was such a shock. But now, with the help of Mr. Baines, our counselor, I feel that we can be reconciled. Margery is *such* a fine person. Such a sensitive human being. Would you like to see a snapshot of her?"

"No," I said, pouring myself some more champagne. "I don't think I would."

"She's a librarian," Harold explained. "Her specialty is children's literature."

I nodded.

"We met in high school. Actually, we were childhood sweethearts."

I knew that if the conversation went on any longer, I was going to lose control. So I got to my feet and went to the hall closet, where my mother's fake fur was hanging. I reached into the pocket and took out Harold's check. "Look . . ." I began.

"Yes?" Harold said innocently.

"There's something here I want to give you."

"Yes?" he said.

Hang in there, my inner voice said. Hang in there, give him the check, and depart. Dignity is everything.

"Mr. Murth," I said calmly, "I herewith present you with a check for a thousand dollars. This money has been raised by, uh, persons who wish to remain anonymous so that you can go to England and finish your thesis. You may consider it a kind of grant."

Harold looked blank. "England?"

"The money is for you to go to England and complete your thesis on Smart," I repeated patiently.

"But my thesis has already been completed," Harold replied. "I completed it last month."

"Without going to Cambridge?"

"But of course. Why should I go to Cambridge?"

I sat down again, the check dangling limply between my fingers. "Look, Mr. Murth, let me give this to you straight. Some time ago I learned from Esther Tilley that you were living in very difficult circumstances and could not get to Cambridge to finish your thesis. Miss Tilley also said that she had typed part of your thesis to help you out and that you were supporting your mother in New Jersey and everything. This money was raised by interested parties to assist you."

Harold looked stunned. "But my dear Miss McAllister, absolutely *none* of that is true."

"It isn't?"

Harold drew his stool nearer to me and wrapped the bathrobe tightly about him. "Indeed, it isn't. Esther Tilley has got everything muddled. How unfortunate."

"Yeah," I agreed. "It is."

"Miss Tilley . . ." Harold said reluctantly. "Well, to be very frank about it, Miss Tilley has a slight drinking problem and tends to get things confused. As for the typing, I gave her the job to help *her* out. She lives very modestly, you know. With her aunt."

"But maybe you could use the money anyway," I said. "For emergencies."

160

A look of embarrassment crossed Harold's face. "My dear child, I am not in need of money."

I gazed at my empty glass and wondered why I wasn't drunk yet. I had finished half a bottle of champagne.

Harold paused and thought for a while. Then he seemed to come to some deep inner decision. "Miss McAllister," he said, "have you ever heard of the Motel Murths?"

Had I ever heard of them? Of course I had heard of them. They were as famous as the Hiltons. "Of course," I said.

"Well," Harold sighed, "that is the family I come from. They own, as you probably know, the Holiday House Motels. So surely you understand that I could go to England if I wished."

"You mean," I said faintly, "that you're rich."

Harold rose to his feet and began to pace the room. "I'm afraid I am, Miss McAllister—but I have never taken advantage of it. I have always lived quite Spartanly, in the manner of a scholar, and avoided the family business. My values have been consistently Greek, in the best sense of the word, and it is my adherence to these values that has caused a slight friction between me and my wife. Melvin Babb, my cousin, has chosen quite a different route, as you probably noticed that night at the play-reading. He uses family funds to advance his career. But, as you said earlier, *c'est la vie.*"

Something very close to hysteria swept through me. "OK!" I said. "Fine! So why is your cousin's name Melvin Babb when he comes from a family of Murths?"

Harold gave me a sweet, almost pitying smile. "Melvin

161

thought that 'Melvin Murth' was not suitable for the theatre. He chose Babb instead—his mother's maiden name."

I tilted the bottle of champagne to my lips and finished it. It tasted like flattened grape juice. "So what you're telling me, Mr. Murth, is that you don't need a thousand bucks."

"That is correct. You must return it at once to the people who raised it. With my profound thanks, of course."

"Of course," I said. "Of course." Suddenly I realized that I was getting a headache.

"I'd better be going," I said. "I don't feel very well."

Harold looked concerned. "May I escort you home?"

"No, no. Have your bath. Enjoy yourself. Merry Christmas."

"I *do* have things to do tonight," Harold said. "Margery is coming over tomorrow and I want to make things festive for her."

I rose to my feet and staggered a little. Dear God, I prayed, don't let me puke. Let me puke when I get home, but not here.

Harold was holding my coat, so I slipped into it. I thought of my clothes, my hairdo, the patent leather shoes, and a silent sob racked my chest. I pretended that it was a cough. "Look . . ." I began.

"Yes?" Harold said cheerfully.

"There's just one more thing I want to ask you and then I'm going to leave. Because quite obviously I am lousing

162

up your Christmas and I don't want to do that. But I do have to ask you one thing."

"But of course," Harold said kindly.

"OK," I said, straightening my shoulders. "What I want to ask you is this. On the last day of school you threw a New York Telephone Company envelope away, on your way to the auditorium, and on this envelope you had doodled my name. I mean, I just happened to see this envelope by accident and wondered why my name was all over it. That's all."

Harold seemed to be racking his brain. "The New York Telephone Company . . ." he muttered. "Let me see. You say it was *your* name I had doodled?"

"Yes. My name."

"Ah ha!" said Harold. "I remember." He blushed. "I hope you won't take this the wrong way, Miss McAllister, but on that particular morning I had been thinking of you. Of your kindness to me when I was ill. And your extraordinary generosity in giving gifts. 'She is a very dear child,' I said to myself, and thus I doodled your name. I hope you don't mind."

"Mind?" I said. "I don't mind a goddamn thing."

Harold looked worried. "Have I offended you in some way?"

For a second I felt laughter rising in me. Mad, crazy laughter. The laughter of Christopher Smart in Saint Luke's Hospital in London. The laughter of a Wall Street tycoon who has just been wiped out.

"Look," I said, "just have a Merry Christmas with your

wife, OK? I'm sorry I barged in on you and I wish you a good New Year."

Harold looked at me—oblivious of my feelings, my future, my grief, the meaning of the gifts I had sent him, the meaning of the thousand dollars . . . in fact, he looked at me oblivious of every fact in the world save that it was Christmas Eve and he would see his wife on the following day. His face was like a child's who has not yet learned that there is evil in the world, a tiny boy who still believes in Saint Nicholas and the tooth fairy.

"Merry Christmas," I said. "And good night."

Unexpectedly, Harold took my hand and held it. "Merry Christmas to *you*, Miss McAllister. And the best tidings of the season. I hope you have a wonderful day tomorrow."

"Oh, I will," I said, smiling brightly. "Don't worry about it. I will."

19

It was Christmas morning and I had decided to commit suicide. The only trouble was, I wasn't exactly sure how to do it. I had no access to sleeping pills, and our oven was electric. Jumping out of windows was not exactly my thing and you could not get carbon monoxide from a bicycle.

"Drowning," I said aloud.

I stared at the clock on my bureau and saw that it was only 6:30. My parents would not be up for hours, and the East River would be deserted at this time of day. Especially on Christmas. I had read somewhere that people who drowned themselves often weighted themselves down with heavy objects—and decided that my Webster's Unabridged Dictionary would do perfectly. But first I had to do one thing.

I unlocked my door and crept into the living room, where our Christmas tree stood in tinseled splendor. Beneath the tree were dozens of presents and there was one that I wanted to open before I died. Marylou's.

I found it at once—a fat oblong box wrapped in silver paper with a satin bow. You give terrific presents, I said in my mind to Marylou. You always have.

I tore off the wrappings and found a chromatic harmonica. Or, to be exact, the Hohner Chromonica 280 in the key of C. It was the one thing I wanted above anything else in the world, and here it was. On the day of my demise.

I realized that I was crying—large, dreadful tears sloshing down my face—so I brushed them away and took the harmonica back to my room. It would do no harm to play it before I left for the East River. I started off with a little Bach.

Fantastic, I thought, as I pressed the lever at the side and created a sharp. Beautiful, I said to myself. I've got to stop smoking again.

But then I realized that I would have no desire to smoke at the bottom of the East River. I went over to my desk and sat down to write a suicide note. "To Whom It May Concern . . ." I began.

A thousand phrases raced through my mind. This life is too difficult for me to bear, and so I have decided to leave. . . . There is no justice on this earth, and thus I am departing. . . . I leave all of my possessions to Marylou Brown, including my bike, because she has been a superlative friend. . . . To my parents I leave a firm "goodbye." . . . The phone rang.

"Hello?" I said. "Who is this?"

"It's me," said Marylou. "Did I wake you?"

"No. Not really."

"I'm sorry to call so early, but I was worried about you. You were out very late."

"Yeah," I said bitterly. "I sure was."

Marylou cleared her throat nervously. "Did everything go all right?"

Suddenly I realized that I could not talk about Harold. To anyone. Ever again. "Yeah," I said. "Fine."

Marylou seemed breathless. "Look, I know it's Christmas and everything, but something has happened that you should know about. It's important."

"What's that?"

"Melvin Babb called my mother last night and asked for your phone number. It seems that he's directing a movie with a part in it for a teen-age girl."

"I thought he was going to direct your mother's play."

"Well, he isn't. They couldn't raise the money. But he *is* going to direct this film called *Catchpenny Road* and one of the parts in it is a girl who looks like a boy. He thought of you right away and wants to interview you this morning."

"You must be kidding."

"I'm not."

"But I'm not an *actor*, Marylou."

"That's exactly what he wants. An unknown."

"An unknown?"

"Someone without experience."

"Wait a minute," I said. "I want to get a cigaret."

I got a cigaret and hurried back to the phone. "Is it a big part?" I asked. "Is the movie going to be made in Hollywood? Who's going to be in it?"

"Slow down," Marylou said. "You haven't got the part yet."

"Well, I'm just curious, that's all. How come he thought of me? How did all this happen?"

"You made a very strong impression on him that night

of the play-reading. It seems that he's never forgotten you."

"Gee," I said. "How amazing. What time should I be there? What should I wear?"

"He wants to see you at noon. In your normal clothes. You know—the Tappan Zee High School outfit."

"Right," I said. "Wow, this is really interesting, isn't it? What did your mother say?"

"She was thrilled."

"Yeah. Man. What an odd turn of events. . . . Oh, *listen*. I opened my present and I love it. It's the best thing you've ever given me."

"You say that every Christmas."

"No, Marylou, I mean it. Did you open yours?"

I had given her a five-year subscription to *Archaeology* magazine.

"Yes. It's wonderful. And Nelson adores his Human Brain set. It's amazing the way the brain lights up and everything."

"Right," I said, "right. Look, I want to take a shower and get my hair back to normal. Should I press my blue jeans?"

"No. He just wants to see the real you."

The real me, I thought. Who is that? It has *got* to be the person who looks like a teen-age cab driver.

"Listen," I said, "Merry Christmas. And give Nelson a hug. I'll call you later."

"Good luck," said Marylou. "I'll be thinking of you at noon."

And so, at exactly twelve o'clock I rang Melvin Babb's doorbell on East End Avenue. He answered it at once—and once again I was startled at how short he was. How fat. He was wearing a maroon silk dressing gown.

He stared at me. "It's too much. I don't believe it."

"Believe what?" I said.

"You are *divine*," he said. "Come in at once."

I came in and stood in the middle of the living room. The apartment—with its plants and antiques, tropical birds and mirrors—was a surprise all over again. With a look of concentration, Melvin circled me. *"Divine,"* he muttered. "Too good to be true."

I felt a little strange standing there in my blue jeans and sneakers and Tappan Zee High School jacket, so I said, "I didn't dress up or anything. I hope it's OK."

Melvin put a plump finger to his lips. "Shhh. I'm thinking."

He continued to circle me, making little noises under his breath. Then he said, "All right. You can sit down now."

I sat on an oversized sofa that faced a view of the river. "You know," I said, "I'm not a trained actor or anything."

"I don't want a trained actor for this film," he said sternly. "What I want is what the French call *un original.* You know what that means?"

I took a cigaret from the coffee table and lit it. "Sure," I said. "Of course."

Melvin smiled. "You are adorable. Tell me something about yourself."

169

"Well . . ." I began. "What would you care to know?"

He winked at me. "Anything you would care to reveal."

"Oh," I said. "OK. Well, I'm a junior in prep school, and I used to be very good at sports except that my smoking got in the way. I'm rather a compulsive person, and a poor student, but I have always prided myself that I understood people. You know?" Melvin nodded.

My mind darted around, wondering what to tell him. "I've had sort of a problem most of my life," I said, "in the sense that very few people like the way I look. Especially my mother. But *I* have always liked the way I looked, so what can you do?"

Melvin nodded sympathetically. "The very best of us have different drummers, my child." Suddenly he glanced at his watch. "Mercy, it's after twelve! You must be famished. What would you like for lunch? A little poached salmon? Some white wine?"

"Sure," I said. "Why not?"

Melvin wafted into the kitchen, gave some instructions to the maid, and wafted out again. In the few moments that he was gone I glanced around the room and saw that his Christmas tree, in the corner, was entirely white. White tree, white decorations, and underneath the tree, several presents wrapped in white. Weird, I said to myself. Really weird.

Melvin settled down in the chair opposite me and gave me a coy smile. "It's *adorable* of you to come over on Christmas Day, so let me fill you in on our project. I'm about to direct a little film called *Catchpenny Road* which

170

takes place in the Depression and which has three main characters—two hoboes called Randall and Jim, and a tomboy named Spunky."

"Is that my part?" I asked.

"If we cast you, yes. Now the idea of the plot is that Randall and Jim are con-artists who travel from town to town in the Middle West. Sometimes they sell bogus encyclopedias and sometimes they cheat people at cards. They sell fake patent medicines, do magic shows, and in general try to swindle everyone they meet. Spunky, the tomboy, is their front. In other words, they use her to soften people up. She has to be very open and appealing—like you—but a crook."

"A crook?"

"Absolutely. A con-artist."

"Oh," I said.

"And then, of course, there's the fact that people take her for a boy—which adds some absolutely *killing* things to the plot."

"Like what?"

"Like a local waitress falling in love with her."

"Oh," I said.

"It's really killing. The waitress, whose name is Mona, has been had by every man in town—and here she is, falling in love with Spunky."

"I see."

Melvin Babb's eyes widened. I realized that he was staring at Echo, my harmonica. My mother had finally given it back, and it was sticking out of the pocket of my jacket. "You don't play the harmonica?" he said slowly.

All of a sudden I felt nervous. "Well, yes," I replied. "I do. In a way."

He put a weary hand to his brow. "This is too much. And all in one morning. I can't bear it."

"I don't understand."

"A *harmonica* in the midst of the whole thing would be sheer heaven," Melvin explained. "The tomboy could play it as a kind of frame for the piece. I mean, it really would be divine. The three of them wandering across America to the sound of a harmonica—the harmonica representing their *joie de vivre*, their random gaiety in the midst of sadness, their funkiness, if I may use such a word. I don't suppose you'd play a few tunes for me, J.F.? Just a tiny audition."

"No," I said. "I won't."

Melvin looked blank. "I beg your pardon?"

"I said I won't play for you," I said loudly. "I'm sorry."

Because all of a sudden it had dawned on me what was happening. What this creep wanted to do was use me. Exploit me. Take the way I looked and make capital of it. This fat phony was going to take me and my Tappan Zee High School outfit and my harmonica and make a fast buck out of them. And it made me want to puke. Here I had thought that he liked me for myself, when the real thing he liked was that I was a freak. Because I *was* a freak, I decided suddenly. I didn't look like anybody else, or sound like anybody else, or act like anybody else. And I never had. I had spent my whole life worrying about being a peculiar person, when that was what I was *meant* to be in the first place. So screw it, I thought furiously. If I am a freak at least I'll be an honest freak and not use my freakiness to become some goddamn movie star. Wow, I thought, life is really terrible. I wouldn't have believed it.

I walked to the door. "I'm going home now," I said to Melvin Babb.

He looked amazed. "But I don't understand. . . ."

"You never will," I said calmly. "So don't worry about it."

Melvin Babb went red in the face, and for a moment he looked like a very fat child who was about to have a tantrum. "Do you realize what you're giving up?" he said tensely. "This film is very likely to win an *Oscar.*"

"I don't care if it wins a Clarence," I said calmly. "Good-bye."

20

I had decided—at last—to reveal myself to Dr. Waingloss. I had evaded him for four months now, and enough was enough. "Dr. Waingloss," I was going to say, "I need your help. The man I love is married to somebody else. I have been thinking of committing suicide. I have just turned down a part in a movie. You are right about my having a severe anxiety-neurosis. It is so severe that I have recently developed a nervous tic, and my smoking is so bad that I have lost my sense of smell. I have had insomnia for an entire week and lost four pounds. I need your help."

The receptionist admitted me at once and I marched into Dr. Waingloss' office, ready to spill the beans. To my surprise, he was standing by the window holding the photograph of the woman who looked like a sheepdog. He didn't even notice me.

"Dr. Waingloss?" I said.

There was no reply.

"Dr. Waingloss?" I repeated. "It's me. J.F. It's time for our session."

He turned and gave me a blank look.

"It's me," I said in a small voice. "J.F."

"Oh," he said vaguely. "Well. How are you today?"

"Fine," I said. "How are you?"

There was no reply.

"I'm not really fine," I confessed. "You see, a couple of things have happened . . ."

But he wasn't listening to me. And the longer I stared at him, the more I realized that he was in a state of shock. I went over and touched his arm. "Dr. Waingloss, what's the matter? You look terrible."

"It's Freda," he said in a muffled voice. "My analyst. She's moving to Chicago."

I sat down on the couch—stunned by the identity of the sheepdog lady. "Your *analyst*?"

"She lives on 86th Street," he said, clutching the photograph. "I see her three times a week and now she's moving."

"You have an analyst?"

"Yes," he replied, averting his head. "I have an analyst."

"A headshrinker?"

"Of course!" he said angrily. "I'm a human being, aren't I? Why does no one think I'm a human being?"

"I think you're a human being," I said. "Honest."

"Why are psychiatrists always treated as though they were tape recorders?" he said furiously. "We have feelings! We suffer! We love!"

"I know," I said, "I know. It's OK, Dr. Waingloss. Everything is going to be OK."

He sat down in the leather chair, his face a mask of grief.

"When is she moving?" I inquired.

"Next month."

"To Chicago?"

"Yes. And I don't know how I'm going to bear it."

I was rather at a loss for words. "Well . . . maybe you could get another analyst and start over. Would that be difficult?"

He stared at me as though I were insane. "*Difficult?* Freda Buchmeister and I have been together for ten years. We are tuned to one another."

"But maybe you could get someone like her."

"There is no one like her," he declared.

"Well . . ." I said lamely. "Why don't you talk about her? It might help."

And so, for the next fifty minutes, Dr. Waingloss and I sat facing each other as he told me about Freda Buchmeister. How Freda Buchmeister had grown up in Vienna and trained with a pupil of Freud's. How she had treated famous people all over the world. How she had once delivered a paper to the American Psychoanalytic Association that had revolutionized the theory of the Oedipus Complex. And the more I listened to him, the more I realized that I could never tell him about Harold Murth, or Melvin Babb, or how I had been contemplating suicide. There was no one to tell—not even Marylou—because these were my problems now, and I had to deal with them.

At the end of the session I shook Dr. Waingloss' hand— because I knew that we would never see each other again—and walked out of the office. I felt terribly empty, but intact, as though I had just survived a natural disaster. I also felt a hundred years old.

I don't remember doing it, but I must have walked all the way across town—to the promenade by the East River on 84th Street. It was a cold gray day, and though I was shivering in my Tappan Zee High School jacket, I didn't care. All I wanted to do was be alone for a while, and think, and not talk to anyone.

There weren't many people around, just three little girls skipping rope, so I sat down on a bench and stared at the river. It was a kind of gunmetal gray, and the little tugboats that passed looked bright and strange. Then I reached in my back pocket and took out Echo, my harmonica. I began to play my World War I medley, very softly, and I was playing for lots of people besides myself. For Nelson, who was such a creep. And for Marylou, who had a crooked smile and bit her fingernails. For Dr. Waingloss, who was in love with his analyst, and for all the bums who panhandled on Fifth Avenue. I was even playing for my mother—because she was a lonely person—and in a place I couldn't bear to think about I was playing for Harold Murth, who had turned out to be so ordinary. Just an ordinary man married to a girl named Margery. In Tenafly, New Jersey.

So I played for a long time, and the tunes I played drifted out over the East River and mingled with the sound of tugboats and the roar of airplanes flying in to Kennedy Airport. And the more I played, the more peaceful I became. I can't explain it, but it was as if I had finally come to terms with something. Or relinquished something. I mean, life wasn't terribly marvelous, but it didn't stink either—the way I had once thought. Life was simply . . . itself. Like me. J.F. McAllister.

Format by Gloria Bressler
Set in 11 point Times Roman
Composed, printed and bound by The Haddon Craftsmen,
Scranton, Pa.
HARPER & ROW, PUBLISHERS, INCORPORATED

Date Due